LETTERS FROM HANUSSE

WORKS BY DOUGLAS MESSERLI

POETRY

River to Rivet: A Poetic Trilogy
Dinner on the Lawn (College Park, Maryland:
Sun & Moon Press, 1979; revised 1982)
River to Rivet: A Manifesto (College Park, Maryland:
Sun & Moon Press, 1984)
Some Distance (New York: Segue, 1982)

Maxims from My Mother's Milk/Hymns to Him
(Los Angeles: Sun & Moon Press, 1988)

An Apple, A Day (Riverdale, Maryland: Pyramid Atlantic, 1993)

After (Los Angeles, Sun & Moon Press, 1998)

primeiras palavras [in Portuguese and English]
(Cortia, Brasil: Ateliê Editorial, 1999)

FICTION, DRAMA, AND MIXED GENRE

Silence All Round Marked: An Historical Play in Hysteria Writ
(Los Angeles: Blue Corner Drama Books, 1991)

The Structure of Destruction
1. Along Without: A Film for Fiction in Poetry
(Los Angeles: Littoral Books, 1993)
2. The Walls Come True: An Opera for Spoken Voices
(Los Angeles: Littoral Books, 1996)
3. Letters from Hanusse [Joshua Haigh]
(Los Angeles: Green Integer, 2000)

The Confirmation [as Kier Peters]
(Los Angeles: Sun & Moon Press, 1993)

Still in Love [an opera; music by Michael Kowalski;
text and scenario as Kier Peters] [disk]
(Dexter, Michigan: Equlibrium, 1997)

Joshua Haigh

LETTERS
from HANUSSE

(THE STRUCTURE OF DESTRUCTION: 3)

*Edited with a Preface
by Douglas Messerli*

GREEN INTEGER
KØBENHAVN

& —————————————

LOS ANGELES
2000

GREEN INTEGER BOOKS
Edited by Per Bregne
København/Los Angeles

Distributed in the United States by Consortium Book
Sales and Distribution, 1045 Westgate Drive, Suite 90
Saint Paul, Minnesota 55114-1065

(323) 857-1115/http://www.greeninteger.com

First Edition 2000
©2000 by Douglas Messerli (Joshua Haigh)
Back cover copy ©2000 by Green Integer

Design: Per Bregne
Typography: Guy Bennett
Cover: Photograph of Joshua Haigh by Howard N. Fox

LIBRARY OF CONGRESS CATALOGING IN PUBLICATION DATA
Messerli, Douglas [Joshua Haigh] 1947
Letters from Hanusse
ISBN: 1-892295-30-X
p. cm — Green Integer 30
I. Title II. Series

ary abilities? Certainly, acquainted as I was with geography, there was no place on my map named Hanusse! I attempted to read the word as an anagram, symbol, metaphor, an imaginary map of an intellect.

To use this text as part of my own ongoing exploration of evil, wasn't that akin to something like plagiarism? Yet, my involvement with Ricochet's texts in the previous two volumes and the incorporation of short sections from fictions of many novelists and the biographies of dictators, hadn't that explored the same territory? The envelope of Haigh's letters represented no return address. He had claimed death. Perhaps I owed him, at least, the publication of his volume, so perfectly aligned with my own concerns, so closely related to what I had already attempted to express.

Read this volume as you will. It is Haigh's fiction or, perhaps, his history, his communication with the world outside of his own—whether it be an imagined world or what we sometimes call a "real" one. I have only edited it, corrected his typographical errors, maintained a certain respect for consistencies of time and place. The links between my previous two volumes and this will be apparent nonetheless. This incredible work, which I had had no time to conceive had come to life out of the very facts that I had felt it necessary to represent through the recreation of the work of the little known French philosopher, biographer, filmmaker, fiction writer, belle-lettrist, a man I encountered only in my youth. Time had doubled back, had created another figure who, like myself, was affected—no *in*fected with the same issues with which I had so long been concerned.

Ever since reading this work, I have had an eerie feeling that there are other people in the world who not only share similar experiences and aspects of personality, but *are* actually me; are people who share my mind, my body, my life. Joshua Haigh, Claude Ricochet, these two particularly. Both now dead as I will eventually be. A kind of unholy trinity: father, son, and ghost. You, dear reader, must determine whom each of us is.

—DOUGLAS MESSERLI

"After dinner the fool began a story that, like all his stories, kept interrupting itself. One tale would begin only to have another spun out of it, and no sooner had the second begun when a third issued from it, and a fourth from that one.

The King grew impatient with the "interruptions" and called over to the fool, "Stop! Finish one story, at least, before embarking on another."

So, said the fool, "I am done."

"With which one? And what happened?" pleaded the exasperated King.

"All of them are the same one," answered the fool, "a tale told before it was begun."

—CLAUDE RICOCHET,
The Structure of Destruction

Where are you now extraordinary creature? The pilgrims have left the city, bought up all the postcards. The pigeons arc bored. Chewing gum covers most of the cement. It's all a little sad. As you know, things here are defined by devout petty motions, their purchases: popcorn, cologne, green ribbons, ice cream, statuettes.

Naturally, I'll remain. Tomorrow I'll go to the bar and read *Scientific American*. I'll be disappointed. The shadows are so short; the breeze has blown out to ocean; all the trees are covered with dust. My asthma is a bother, of course. Perhaps I'll bicycle out to the old dance hall, if I can breathe a bit.

But these are only speculations. I still inhabit an empty house. True, Mrs. Velde has tried to make me happy. She never tires of cooking (the rooms smell eternally of bacon fat). She has hung lace curtains on the windows. She's scrubbed the floors. She's even offered, flat hand extended, to grace the spot of floor I call my bed. But I have refused—the children are back!

Minnie has grown so tall. She has yellow hair. Yesterday she burned the spinach—the entire crop. Evidently she thought I was growing some mind-expanding plant. Such a moral child. Like you. Like her father and mother. I try to corrupt her a little from time to time, but so far without success. Always angelic, keeping her troubles to herself and that wretched doll Minerva. Did you know she had her painted red? It's a warning, I suspect. Whenever I come near her she puts the doll between us and gyrates her shoulders and head as if possessed.

Ford is so different. Runs around, the long-haired little darling, stark-raving naked. Rummages the garbage for whatever—an egg-shell, an empty beer glass— which he can bring me as an offering I guess. For weeks now he has brought his little overtanned body down to sleep with mine. Not that I've regretted it. But he's such a demon! Slips out in the deep of every night. God knows where he is going or where he has been when, just before daylight, he sneaks back. He is like that cat we had in Jackson Heights. Remember? The one that jumped from a windowsill too high to live?

Do you have a new cat? Who are these "friends"? I've attempted to imagine you in London—or is it Florence? I heard you were traveling, and I've tried to picture you first in fog, then in Italian sun. I simply can't. I've never been anywhere except Jackson Heights. They call me "the native" to tease, but I'm proud of this silly epithet. I am what they say. How few can admit to that? I'm here and I'm always here, and it makes me somewhat happy. This clumsy excuse for a road into town lined with stubborn nut trees, this Hanusse—a shantyville at best—this half-collapsed summer house: I can see them in memories of the future and past. So you must forgive me if I can't grasp your situation. In London or Florence—or maybe it was Venice where I was told you went—do they have berries as black?

I think Leon was correct. We demand our own environments. I'm curious, however, not having gone as you have, the limit. I see it as an accident. I've always been rather passive as when you tore up my drawings without my really minding much. I have only a collage left, and it reminds me of me and what you've done. It's all green except for two torn shreds of paper pasted to the center, a face in obvious anguish and a word ripped in half: *acci,* like some sort of guinea phrase. Does it mean anything? I think originally it was *accident* or *accidental,* although I can't be sure. It could have been *accipter,* which is the family name for hawks. I can't think of anything else it might have been. But, you see, that isn't the point. It isn't any of them. It isn't anything actually, unless it *does* mean something in Italian. I think this is what happened to us.

…If anything happened to us. As you'll recall, I'm not very good at figuring these things out. And here I've grown even more simple-minded. I like being in a house alone or with a boy, or with a boy and a girl and a hausfrau if it has to be, and you know how I hate wearing shirts and shoes and sometimes pants. Clearly, I'm not very civilized. For instance, you should see my toenails! I keep forgetting to have Mrs. Velde give me a trim. You used to do it so well! Always reminding me of things like that.

But I've embarrassed you. I know you well enough or did once. You have my permission to burn this. If only I had some Milk of Magnesia. Do you think you could send some? That's all I ask.

Ah, but I won't have you think this is paradise! We have no plumbing, no sanitaries whatsoever! There is from Hanusse a constant effluence of stench! And oh how you would tremble at the insects! They are gradually eating away our flesh! Minnie is immune: a strong body's defense. But Ford and I are obviously weaker. They torment us: the jiggers, the brown-clock spiders, the horseshoe beetles, the centipedes. They're everywhere. We can't comfortably sleep (perhaps Ford's night wanderings *are* the answer). Recently they captured the coffee sack!

We *have* learned to purify the water, but it is such an endless task. Mrs. Velde is forgetful, scrubbing and cooking and stamping at the vermin, so the boiling pot is mostly neglected, evaporated up. In this way we some days lose pot after pot.

And we have no refrigeration, so our meats must be spiced. We use coriander, cumin, dried red peppers and salt, when it looks relatively pure of cockroach. My stomach has behaved valiantly, but is always *near* revolt. Perhaps you should include some Kaopectate. I have enclosed a check from what is left of my American account.

* *
*

Drink, reading, exercise—all are out. It has been raining now for several hours. Minnie, seeing it coming, repaired to the veranda. (I wish I could prefer her as you would. I pray she's not hopelessly "nice." She plays the guitar on which I count [O music! steal her heart!].) And Mrs. Velde has had a vision: Ford is engulfed in the mud! I'm a little upset, for he did not return at dawn, and she has psychic powers much admired in Hanusse. Did your mother really know I was going to ring at exactly 5:00? Suddenly it seems so important to have the truth, a matter of living out the afternoon. The soil is so porous! There is some relief in the fact that he is only thirteen and weighs perhaps too little for the mud to suck him in.

It's already clear that Hanusse is a disaster. Has it ever not been? It can't really be said to have been built or settled—even "envisioned." For hundreds of centuries it remained wild, with perhaps a new hut added every other decade, which could hardly have been expected to survive constructed of mud and grass. The tribes of New Guinea were certainly more advanced. No history, no artifacts—how it frustrates anthropologists! How to explore the ruins of something that didn't exist but *was* nonetheless? If the climate were only a degree or two cooler; if the coconuts hadn't come crashing to ground in the winds of each monsoon; if the stalks of sassafras, anise, red thyme and sorrel hadn't overrun the plains about: what would we have been? Another China? Another Japan? Things become easy. The French conquer, the Spanish plunder, the pilgrims leech. Assimilation is the simplest of tasks.

The history we know is rather simple: Magellan is believed to have overlooked us. But this is not certain (we are such an unsure folk), for the local priest insists that the blood of Magellan courses through the veins of the people which, he explains, is why the Hanussee speak French. No one here has dared to contradict him, and I'm the only one who's learned that Magellan was Spanish (?), am I right? (Increasingly my schoolbook memory fails me. I've forgotten even how to subtract.)

The priest, however, might not entirely be mistaken, for it's not really French the natives speak but a blend of French and Spanish of which I know only a few words, having never bothered to imitate. You see how lazy I've been? But it really doesn't matter. English functions just as well. Not *your* English, of course, but a breed of it, like the meat, spiced.

I've told you before most of what I know of this language, but did I mention that all declensions have been elimated, that there is no distinction between masculine and feminine, that the differentiation between personal pronouns has been lost? He is my aunt she is my father are common constructions. Proper nouns have therefore come to be heavily stressed. You wouldn't like it I imagine. The repetition of your name—such a wonderful name too, although you hate it—Hannah Hannah Hannah would drive you off. Remember the boy at the bus stop and how I laughed?

O Hannah Hannah Hannah, what should I do? Ford has turned me into such a serious old man. I so worry over him. Maybe it's just the atmosphere. The Hanussee have no sense of humor. They seldom even smile, but they just as seldom seem depressed. I suspect it's the equilibrium of the sun. Except for these seasonal torrents, the daily sun swings so directly into our lives. Nine o'clock is cooler by only a few degrees than noon, when the temperature often reads 38. The sun is called Souil, and is the hero of a myth far more revealing than the history I've begun in order to distract myself.

One day Souil was lonely in the clouds, so it's said. Before this day Souil had always been contented as a bachelor with the stars for friends.

From the wet skirts of earth (Ter) Souil had always remained aloof. But today she-he descended on a journey in seach of something different.

When Ter saw Souil approach she-he was aghast: how unprepared was Ter for a visit such as this. Ter's wet skirts dried up and disappeared wherever Souil turned her-his face to her-him. And how surprised was Souil to see beneath the waters new fantastic lands. Souil traveled long and far in wonderment. Gradually, however, Souil tired and sank into waters for a rest. There also the waters dried and land showed a new face. But how more lovely, more lush was *this* compared with the rest.

What is your name, Souil asked. Obviously frightened by such attentions, the land whispered Oodi. Observing this, Souil posed another riddle: Why are you afraid? I am afraid that you are too much for me, that in your love I will be burned to a crisp. Souil understood and spoke: Regretfully, I must leave you, but I will return to watch you playing in the waters from afar.

And true to her-his word, Souil had continued
to come back.

*   *
*

It took the French to manufacture us: 550 slave Moroccans, 100 Legionnaires. They backpacked it:
lacework grilles, embroidered silk, cotton, marble, religion, beads and rugs. Mohammed knows why they
chose this place to set it down. Like Souil, I suppose,
they were simply exhausted. Once they *had* relieved
their backs, however, there was nothing on earth to
convince to stoop and bear again. And Souil—visiting
as usual—was so dreadfully intense:

The silks were slowly shrinking,
the rugs were fading fast,
one by one the soldiers started to collapse...

(the natives sing this in the classroom). A child would
have had the sense to build a shelter; the French erected
two, a dozen, more. Suddenly a city had been raised.
The Moroccans were amazed at what they'd helped to
accomplish, and the *capitaine* had the good sense to

award them the choice of a name for it: how could they know that it already had a name for itself?

And before the meaning of Hanusse could be determined, the Spanish came rushing in. The French, it seems, had stolen the Moroccans from some sultan, and the Spaniards were outraged on his behalf. To prove it they raped and shot all but one of the Legionnaires—a man who incredibly intrigues me. Was he *that* grotesque? Or beautiful? Or willing? Or blessed? There are always rumors, and I believe all of them!

Don't be alarmed! My continual confusion (wasn't it "messy pluralism" Leon called it?) was proven impractical in New York and, I imagine, would be equally unsuitable for life in London or Italy or wherever you're at. No doubt it *is* "villainous" or "savage" or "a mere affectation" or—my favorite—"further evidence of a mediocre mind's collapse" (isn't it frightening how the mind retains these things?), but was it worthy of such abandonment? I've seen Leon, but they shouldn't have permitted it. I'm not reporting this to torment —you know how I detest your guilt!—I only want to understand. Why wasn't I affected like Leon, Lizzie— even you? Was the Frenchman confused enough in the end to grasp at rumors of himself? What kind of "truth" could he bring back?

*

Thank God Ford has returned, muddily amused by all our fears for him. He says the road to town is out, meaning we'll be forced to rely upon what's left of our garden for a few months. The yams can be saved perhaps, and Mrs. Velde thinks she might rescure the burdock. Have you ever eaten it? Mrs. Velde includes it in her deep-fried pancakes:

> 1 carrot, shredded (DO NOT PARE)
> 2 5-centimeter pieces of shredded burdock
> 45 grams shredded ginger
> 142–170 grams scallops
> 2 eggs
> ¼ liter flour

> Combine ingredients and vigorously whip.
> Pour into griddle and flip.

You should hazard it. It tastes somewhat like cayenne-flavored paste. But it is filling, and if you're near starvation, actually quite good.

Yes, occasionally we go hungry for a few days at a spell. But it's not the same as suffering. We don't even mind it much. Our minds are kept busy with amusements. We don't go about the countryside *all* poker-faced! Why, on our evening walk we came upon a band of wild gorillas encircling a donkey near the woods just the other night. There was the donkey, braying braying in absolute terror. Even Minnie dropped her jaws a mite.

Oh Hannah, don't accuse! We were merely curious. Like the night Leon was attacked. He was more horrified by your interest in the assailant, I think, than he was by the assault. How silly of him! Doesn't everyone know that if you throw a man off a roof you'll get an audience?

Mrs. Velde has never seen a murder, much to her disappointment. Not even an attempted one! Her sister, however, lives in San Francisco and writes letters which describe in exacting detail old Perry Mason and detective-story plots. Obviously thrilled with these narratives of death Mrs. V consequently is prone to hallucinations (which, I suppose, is related to her gypsy-powers), during which she insists she is being followed, watched, stalked and otherwise in danger of some sort of molestation (which may have more to do with her desire to sleep with me than sex). It's her damn persuasiveness which I resent. She's convinced Ford, for example, to walk her to the well at the very moment I've run a sponge down his legs. He's usually wise to her tricks. But please, she cajoles him, I have a message from the bloody one: I embrace you in the rains of night (I gather it was "the reigns of night" in which the murderer embraced his victim in the book. Does such a phrase bring to mind one of your Dorothy Sayers, Agatha Christie, Geoffrey Household?). Ford scoffs, and turns to her, obviously aroused by my attentions. You are skeptical, she says, then what of this?—and out from under her apron she pulls a pig fetus. It was lying at the door, she rebukes. Off Ford trots! And this too amuses me—although I'm peeved a bit.

I realize I've long ago reached the point of your incredulity. A domestic can never comprehend how inately bizarre behavior is (has to be) in such forgotten spots! A normal man never stays in an outpost. You run around and say such revolutionary things; he rips the womb apart with his fists! Not intentionally, of course. He will only speak the status quo. A birth is a birth but it isn't: it's a possibility for more than the submissive posture pounded into him. And if in the end he worships Hammurabi's Code, The Ten Commandments—whatever else—it's because he's so close to where he started from. High in welded I-beams you're safe to play with the passions he so desperately fights off.

*   *

*

Scusami for last night! Must have been the burdock or the worry over Ford and mud. One of our worst problems was my vituperativeness. Today let me speak of the Hanusse so prettily framed by tourist snapshots...

Minnie comes creeping over to watch me write. She doesn't understand what a word is, for I refuse to have her learn it. Why should she be taught that this is *pink* when the baskets in the harbor are filled with pink and yellow and blue fish? These *fish* have nothing to do with the men laying them out on the beach. And this *beach* has never felt the dressed and naked children gather in the surf to capture seaweed. I'd prefer she stay illiterate than to think of these as lines of ink. May Souil grant that, like the white-scarved women who stroll down to harbor each afternoon to barter and buy dinner, she take home something real to eat.

I'm the foolish one. I run out. I knock on strange doors, and in every room I find a crucifix. I remind myself of those little black-scarved women with pails and curved iron spoons, collecting insects from the cacti hereabout. When you pass, they refuse to look up. (Yet they weave amazing floral carpets from pieces of corn cob, cane, date pits and soil each Spring.)

Fortunately, Minnie hasn't my imagination, and I must protect her from contracting some. Potatoes grow in the dark. These signs, Minnie, are dangerous things. Keep away! Think instead of that sow we saw sleeping on orange peels in the shade, of Pierre and his bull who thinks he's a cow, of the bright engine red you have turned Minerva's face. But put the doll down, for God's sake! You look like you're performing voodoo rites!

*

But I was speaking of the Hanusse you've read so much about: that package of desirable undesirable lies. It's even in the Almanacks:

95% Roman Catholic, 4% Islamic, 1% aetheist. In Hanusse: La Cathredala Madre Maria, La Cathredala Jesus Christos, the Mosque. Rites of Mary, mother of Jesus, May 31–June 3. The Holy Steps: 8:00 AM–10:00 PM, March 1–August 31. In Carmo: La Cathredala San Germino. Festival de San Germino, June 5–9. The Holy Steps: 8:00 AM–8:00 PM, year round. In Megos: La Cathredala San Megos.

I've always loved the way truth is covered up by facts. Have you ever heard the story of the rapes of Rheon? Now Rheon is a very conservative community. Prosperously fat fathers, and mothers who scurry about to lock up their daughters whenever a male comes within fifty yards of the house. Well, in 1910 there was suddenly a rash of pregnancies among these maidens, and when put to bed with labor pains each laid claim to a virgin birth. The mothers all agreed that their daughters were truly saints. So came the Church to investigate, and wonder of wonders, verified the immaculacy of these dears. For it was proven that none had been near a man since puberty. Moreover, as proof of these miracles—so the Church investigator wrote—we have evidence that each girl was visited several months prior to the birth by a contralto-voiced Sister of Providence, surely an angelic messenger sent from God Himself.

So it is in Hanusse. I guess it really depends on how you define a Roman Catholic. Is it mere genuflection, ashes, abstinence and all that? Because, you have to realize, the Bishop of Hanusse knows no Latin nor English nor French—nor even the language of Hanusee itself. He can't even read in fact! So he's rather hard put when it comes to Biblical texts. You see, we've never had a Bishop who knows anything but what has passed down by tongue through the centuries since the missionaries first came to us. Ordination? Well, Hanussees have never understood that it might be expected of them. Actually, Hanusse knows nothing of Catholicism beyond the borders of its own soil. And you must keep in mind that we are Spanish and French, that absolutely terrifying mystical-egotistical mix—with a dash of Arab madness yet! Flagellation is highly respected. Emasculation not unheard of. Do you understand? When it comes to faith, we are a rather barbaric sect.

And what of the tourists, you might ask? Doesn't their religiosity brush up against our pagan rites? Ah, but don't you see, the tourists adore our sackcloth sanctimoniousness. They think it quaint—wouldn't dream of uttering a peep that might break up the picturesque composition—the nail hammered palms, the blood-raw knees, the pained dismemberment—of their photographs.

Mrs. V tells of the time a couple from Connecticut paid her brother to climb the Cathedral steps of San Megos as they'd seen another do it the day before. The other had had himself pulled up the steps by a rope—knotted round his neck. Mrs. V's brother was very poor.

I see you now slapping this letter to desk, drumming those long painted fingers across the words which have brought you to frustration once again. Why don't you just give me up? For as you see, I've gotten worse: sardonicism increasingly controls my life. Incidentally, do you know the etymology of that word? The Sardinian plant Sardonius, when ingested, affects the respiratory system, causing a series of wheezing explosions such that a victim sounds as if he's laughing at the very instant of death. Don't go to Sardinia, dear, and you'll be all right. In fact, perhaps you should return to the u.s. I can't help but feel a bit uneasy when I think of you being in the land of Mafiosos, Fascists and pinched buttocks.

*

And where are you now?

We have been locked away here—first day by day, most recently hour by hour growing more and more irritable with ourselves. Mrs. Velde so misses her gossip and I my paper and Indiablack that together we might have slit our throats from boredom had it not been for the children, who, as the brunt of our collective attentions, have been caused to crave what they once might have described as our extraordinary lack of parental insticts. Wherever did Mrs. V so suddenly learn the role of the Big Black Mamma and I the Imperious-but-Doting Pappa. I'm convinced that Minnie and Ford would themselves have taken razor to our previously spared necks if Mrs. V once more hugged her "darlings" to bosom or were I to snake my arms round their shoulders and so much as move my tongue in the direction of yet another *obiter dictum*. Fortuitously the workers finally have come and dug us out! Hurrah and all that! And blessing of blessings they have brought our mail and a necessities kit. Mrs. V has sixteen letters to keep her busy, I only one—and that merely a commericial invitation—but the blank back of that message and a box of black shoe cream have brought me to ecstasy. It hardly matters that I have no news of you, alas.

But at least now you shall have news of me; or I should say I will have news of myself. For I'm certain you shall never write me back. How could you? I have been so foolish to think you might. I'm not only uncivilized and sardonic, but oh such a sentimentalist! As if letters should have gone eternally flying in all directions. Why don't I get it into my head that we survived a disaster that was special only because it happened to us? What interest could "the world" sensibly have in three—possibly four—silly sexually confused adolescents? I suspect what I really can't get used to is the fact that "we" are no longer "us," that we too are now "the world," and should have long since lost interest in what happened save for a kind of vague, half nostalgia, half disgust old memories call up.

It's time to shave my beard and chuckle over it. The road is open and my legs are stiff. Besides, the children are desperate for a loneliness.

*   *

*

About 20 kilos from the asylum where Leon lies strapped to his bed, is an ordinary gully, on the edge of which sits a dilapidated quonset hut. This is the retreat of which I've written—a sanctuary so absolute that, since the day I first chanced upon it, its door-jamb has not been crossed by another boot.

Like you—like anyone—I was convinced such quietude could not exist, that my finding it abandoned was coincidental, a slipping in between tourists or behind local peasants who'd perhaps the day before or even just that morning shifted downstream to another hunting spot. Six, seven returns with no indication of intrusion couldn't persuade me. On the eighth, I began the experiments. Just a few well-placed twigs, a strip of bark nailed across the doorcrack; later, chalk sprinkled down the halls, inobvious seashells laid round the perimeter of the hut. It was only wind that scattered the chalk; not a seashell was cracked.

There's something sinister about such seclusion. You find yourself staying for longer numbers of hours, greater stretches of days. You set up kitchen; from an outback pile of half-burnt rubbish, you drag in a mattress, a springless couch, a clock. You strip and go about entirely naked, pissing and ejaculating on the floors, on that slip of cement you've come to call "the patio," on the brown surrounding grass. Eventually you dress and sit up half the night to mimic the cries of monkeys, toucons, cows, pigeons, peacocks, hogs, horses, squirrels, spitting cobras, emmus, and the undomesticated and domesticated dogs and cats.

It's hard to explain actions like that. It has something to do with the walls, the air, the dust—with the sudden realization that you've retreated to one of the most desolate places on the face of the earth, that you might as well have set up camp on the Pleaides or Pluto perhaps.

This is the old dance hall. At least I've been told, by the mailman, that that's what it was, although it's hard—no impossible—to imagine it filled with dancers or to comprehend why anyone ever would have wanted to come this far out from town to dance. I wanted it to be romantic, probing my informer: Why does no one ever go there? Is it haunted? Is there some legend connected with the spot? He was perplexed. Who should go there? The tourists have gone away. There's no one left to dance.

When I was a child, my father sat me down to table and declaimed: We are failed barbarians, my son. We carry battle scars of our perpetual wars with the world in our blood. Every acre is a victor to whom we must bow; but if it gives so much as an inch, we seize it, brand it with a flag, a olive tree or two, and a temporary shack. And that is why, in the end, a field is simply a field, but a house is something you must respect.

I was ten and I thought he was posing a riddle or telling a parable like the tale of the boy who ran away from home to live with the pigs. In later years, I attributed this outburst—one of dozens—to my father's predilection for philosophical tripe. But twenty-seven years after, I've come to understand that it really was a riddle of sorts, a puzzle which my ignorant mailman instantly had figured out.

The Roumanian popularizer, Mircea Eliade, has written:

> The house is not an object, a "machine to live in"; *it is the universe that man constructs for himself by imitating the paradigmatic creation of the gods, the cosmology.* Every construction and every inauguration of a new dwelling are in some measure equivalent to a *new beginning*, a *new life.*

34

That current rage of the French intellectuals, Claude Ricochet, more succinctly explains it:

> The surest signifier of an advanced civilization is a culture's willingness to convert, cut away, tear down, or blow itself up. By contrast, primitive societies—even the nomadic—investing the structures which provide their protection with value (*la qualité*)—anthropormorphise, humanize, and ultimately sanctify the constructions in which they work and play.

But the postman said it best: A dance hall's never not a place to dance.

*

This is the essay that got me an F in my Queen's College freshman composition class:

On Solitude

> There was a man beset by foes, another by catastrophes in daily life. My enemies surround me, suck me of my pleasure, and fling me off like a fig-skin to rot, said the first to his wife; I suffer so, I must fight. And off he went to sue his

adversaries one by one. The second, having been deprived by plague of his entire family, spoke to no one, and retreated into silence like a Carmelite. The first found his coffin within the month; the second survives even as I write.

Now, one might ask of the widower's endurance: What was the result? Some say he's in perpetual pain; others, he's in ecstasy; a few insist he alternates. In short, his condition is incomprehensible to us. Yet does one imagine such sensations in a boy about to be bar mitzved or the maiden soon to discover drops of blood about her cunt. Of course not! For these are about to join us, and we all know where they're soon to be, even if we have forgotten whence they've come. Were either the virgin or her brother to lock himself away, however, how quickly we would cluck: She's nervous; he's hatching up some plot.

As Juvenal teaches: Two things only the mob anxiously awaits: bread and circuses. The former it consumes; the latter it creates.

So it is with me at Tin-Turned Abbey—the nickname with which I've blessed my tin-plated hatch. One minute I am all wrapped up with myself, so enraptured of my isolation that I cannot resist making love to my body parts: I listen attentively while dining to each chomp of my gums; I feel sympathetic to my esophagus' recontre with the Reisling; with adoration I ogle at my swelling stomach—until suddenly—having flattered even my flatulents—I'm sick of it all and desperately desire a crowd to come and lead the beast off.

I wait and wait.

*

How long before it's too long for me to return to normalcy? In the meantime I return to what I can. I enter the kitchen, clear my throat, and toss an onion in the pot. Mrs. V pecks me on the neck so delightfully that I am sorely tempted to reverse the verb and object right there on the floor for your godson. I get as far as my knees, in fact, but the V throws carrots at the stew so insistently that I'm distracted and forget what I'm doing, and before I can remember, Ford is out the door and off. If only we had chairs perhaps he would sit for a second and I be appeased for a month.

In New York I was a pervert, but here I'm not. In Hanusse, where almost everyone "turns the other

37

cheek," so to speak, what you describe as "normal" sex is practiced only by the tourists and the very devout—both of whom, because they pay and pray for us, we forgive and generally forget. As for almost everything that others can't or don't care to comprehend, we have a phrase to express it to ourselves: An apple's to be eaten while a pear's to be plucked.

The Greeks once may have understood, but I'm not even sure of that. Their pederasty was so tutelary, so tied to the protection of daughters and the public pubescence of sons. In Hanusse homosexuality—if you can call it that—is more likely to have been generated by our attempts to keep our boys "down on the farm" in both the metaphoric and the literal sense. You know what they say of harem wives: She who is satisfied never knocks so never knows the door is locked. My countrymen have always recognized that it's easier to leave a table than a bed. So the mother milks her maid-in-waiting, the father fucks his future farmhand, and everyone is happy in the end.

It's a lot like the attitudes of you Americans turned outside in. You love to keep your kiddies innocent because it's how you conceive yourselves as adults. I'll never forget the time we witnessed a citizen of Queens chasing his wife or whoever she was with flying fists down the block. I didn't do anything! I didn't do anything! she screamed as she ran; while he cried: She made me do it! She made me do it! after. Billy the Kid and Al Capone are loveable in your myths. Only outsiders are evil—the "Commies," "the Jews," and—because their skin refuses to erase their origins—the "Orientals" and "Blacks."

*   *
*

I'm not suggesting that *I* have ulterior motives in buggering the little ones; for me, it's simply lust. But I do believe such behavior makes perfect sense. For inevitably, your offspring, seduced by experience, will escape the idyll of your house—at least until guilt and nostalgia draws them in to their own imaginary Edens of Des Moines, Durham, Fort Worth, and Platte. While the apples of our eyes, seeing nothing on the outside they cannot have within, stay to parent us back into the womb from which our generic ancestors sprung. And so it is in Hanusse that brother and sister throughout their lives live as one. Which, I suspect, is why there's no gender in these here parts.

I know what that cowgirl brain of yours is about to ask: How do we breed? Does the father, sick one day of sonny, jump upon the daughter, the son upon his mother, the brother upon his sister, the sister upon a horse? Let me share what Sir Thomas Dale, on his way to Virginia, observed of us when the winds blew him here in 1598:

> Thee most wondresse & amazing Tribe of Natifs ever witnessed came out to greete our approache. Wailing Women stood alle 'pon the Beache & shrieked as each Sailor strode the Gangplanke, and, most surprisingly came to us on Lande to lay their Hands 'pon our Netherparts. Some Meene pulled away but Several stayed to suffer each Caress & Stroke. Many were the Wretches who, lonely for their Wifes, could not themselfes containe, & on these sande Stretches fell into the Handes of Satans Sinne. Hunus I wast told is the pagan Landes Name. And its Peple I surmise are sprung from Atila—the horrible Hun.

What the old governor had witnessed was a rite as ancient as our race. The Seductresses' Rape. It is our greatest—our only—contribution to civilization's course. *We were Circe.* And it is on these shores that,

40

for centuries, men, metamorphosed into swine, bit the dust.

Before the rise of those august institutions that tell people where to go and arrange for them to get there, a girl generally could expect to encounter a member of what you call the opposite sex for one or two months in her entire life. Now, of course, in these liberated days, she can count on one or two months a year. And while once upon a time she proffered her services for nothing but the chance that the stranger's semen might, as we put it, potently infect her, our women now have come to expect financial remuneration and a baby both.

When you compare this method of reproduction with those of other countries, it is really quite ingenious. I mean, you'd think the British would be bored of their horse-faced infants, the Swedes sick of their sunny-headed young, and even the Italians irritated—a little at least—with their black-buttocked boys, as beautiful as they become. All are doomed to repetition, each generation genuflecting through their genes to the next. We, on the other hand, are unconditionally diverse. The face of Hanusse is the face of the earth.

*   *
     *

For your perusal, I have enclosed—based on my readings of Domenico de Rubels, Honrat Nisquet, Francesco Torreblanca, Ludovicus Vlves, Pompeio Sarnelli, Lorenzo Shifreen, Giuseppe Rossi, Jacques Permetti, and Johann Casper Lavater—a physiognomy of Hanusse facial types.

THE FORMS OF THE JAW

The Embryotic Lower Jaw: from the lower lip a backward slope to the neck, so radically receding that the jaw scarcely exists [See the Apes]

The Infantile Jaw: a lower jaw lacking curvature, bony and and obtuse [See the Idiot]

The Dyspeptic Jaw: a jaw perpendicular from the malar to the chin [See the Countess of Huntington]

The Weak Jaw: a short and obtuse jaw, terminating in a receding chin [See Oliver Goldsmith]

The Consumptive Jaw: a generally narrow jaw, pointing up the flatness of the molar bones to a razor-sharp nose that returns the eye to a thin lower lip [See Mimi]

Cardinal Fesch

The Crafty Jaw: a jaw set slightly perpendicular to a sharpened chin [See Laurence Sterne, Voltaire, and Cardinal Fesch]

The Artistic Jaw: a greatly curved jaw set in a rounded face [See Lord Byron, James Hogg, and Elizabeth the First]

The Dramatic Jaw: a jaw terminating in an oval [See Claude Lorraine]

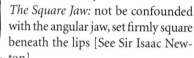

Sir Isaac Newton

The Square Jaw: not be confounded with the angular jaw, set firmly square beneath the lips [See Sir Isaac Newton]

The Contrary Jaw: a lower jaw decidedly angular at the junction of the ramus and the side of the jaw itself [See Voltaire again]

The Prognathous Jaw: an outward inclination of the upper jawbone and a protrusion of the teeth and lip [See Heathens]

SEVERAL SORTS OF CHINS

A. Forms

The Globose: a chin defined by fat

The Oval: a chin dominated by the muscle

The Square: a chin to which the bone gives shape

B. Positions

The Perpendicular; The Receding; The Projecting

A. Lower Lips

The Chef

The Gustatory Lip: a full, pro-trusive, red, moist lip [See the Chef]

The Sociable Lip: a very full lower lip, that, when set in motion, burns bright red [See the Gossip]

The Gossip

The Linguistic Lip: a bright, healthy, limpid lip, moist within [See the Pedant]

The Witty Lip: a lip with a depression set pre-cisely in the center [See the Comic; the Quick Quipster, the Wit]

The Benevolent Lip: a full, normal-colored, ex-tremely wet lip [See the Monk]

The Criminal Lip: a disproportionately small, thin lip or its reverse [See the Lawyer and the Politician]

The Stupid Lip, a lip measuring one-half size of the mouth [See the Journalist]

The Destructive Lip: a lower lip that curves

downward out to reveal the canines [See that you stop him]

B. Upper Lips

The Undeveloped Lip: a thin, flat white lip that presses down the line of closure of the mouth [See the Adolescent]

The Philoprogenitive Lip: a lip that droops downard at either side of its center [See the Father]

The Modest Lip: a lip with a deep groove or channel that divides it into parts [See his Wife]

The Wife

The Imitative Lip: a relatively short upper lip with a curve inward [See his Son]

The Secretive Lip: a lip pointing downward at the center to overlap or close off the cleft of the mouth [See his Mistress]

The Mistress

The Amative Lip: a lip of which the center is extremely full, red and moist [See his Imagination]

The Mirthful Lip: a lip curving upward in an arc [See his Friends and Confidant]

THE CHEEKS

The Globose Cheek: a cheek full, globular, somewhat puffed out [See the Cherub]

45

The Gluttonous Cheek: a full, round cheek which hangs in soft folds upon the neck and breast [See Napoleon and Louis XIV]

The Artistic Cheek: an oval cheek, full to flat [See John Wilkes Booth]

The Conscientious Cheek: a slightly rounded cheek belonging to the square chin type [See Abraham Lincoln]

The Dimpled Cheek: a cheek with a soft, fatty depositon of Andipose material [See Venus]

The Consumptive Cheek: an extremely hollow cheek [See August Strindberg and Isak Dinesen]

The Dyspeptic Cheek: a cheek that collapses inward to reveal the teeth [See Leon in the Clinic]

The Criminal Cheek: a chaotic, soft, flabby, and repulsive-looking cheek [Remember Me, at least]

THE NOSE

Forms: *Concave; Straight; Convex*
Widths: *Narrow; Medium; Wide*
Heights: *Flat; Medium; High*
Lengths: *Short; Medium; Long*
Nostrils: *Narrow; Oblong; Round*
Positions: *Horizontal; Upward; Downward*
Tips: *Pointed; Round; Beveled*
Consistency: *Soft; Flexible; Bard*

Color: *Pale; Mottled; Red*
Functions: *Breathing; Motion; Circulation*

THE EYES

The Agreeable Eye: an eye with a slight downward curve [See Me at breakfast]

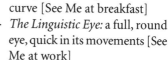

The Linguistic Eye: a full, round eye, quick in its movements [See Me at work]

The Politic Eye: an agreeable eye with an oblique appearance

At work

[See Me at tea]

The Untruthful Eye: an eye turned extremely downward [See Me at supper]

The Inscrutable Eye: an elongated eye with a very narrow slat [See Me later that night]

At supper

The Inquisitive Eye: an eye in which the corners are acute [See Me following the midnight movements of Ford]

The Polygamic Eye: an eye curved into a perfect pod [See Me upon Ford's return near morning]

The Conjugal Eye: a rounded Polygamic Eye, with

47

a slight upward curve [See Me as I rise to waken my sleeping son]

I have left the hair to its barbers and the ears to those who listen to such stuff.

)(

It's clear, my dear, you'd never have the patience to describe the ears, their folds and flaps. It's difficult to see a head, moving at the speed of light. And you Americans are always on the run.

It never ceases to astound me how thoroughly throughout this shrunken century you Americans have sought, in your scurrying about, to assimilate all human types. As if the Eskimo iglooed in your own back yard was not at all an odd fellow but simply was a member of Kiwanis Club, you refuse to recognize those very distinctions which separate a school of sardines from an academy of naval science. How you revel when the Tanganyikan shares his enthusiasm for the Brooklyn Bums (I just remembered that lovely epithet. Do you recall when the Bums beat the pants off—as Leon put it—the Chicago White Socks, 5 to 1?). You Yanks will never be satisfied until everyone, with a self-imposed smile, says I'm an *a merry kin.* To be a melting pot, however, is not to be a laundromat. Steam and press the race as you might, there's always a crease or two left, an eye too high, a nose that draws attention to its toes. And that, my little chickadee, is why the weasel wants you for his lunch.

*

Or did—once. Now that you've flown the coop, he feeds on other fowl like that ugly duckling Lizzie hatched. Even as he writes he watches her erect what proposes to be a lawn chair in a field of waist-high grass. Planting her legs into turf, she kicks up dust, settles back to terra firma, kicks, and lays them in the little furrows they've created. This is not a dance— although her toes push rhythmically against the skin of her shoes. It's like a kind of meditation: with absolute emphasis she has fixed her eyes on the horizon, on some distant point in time like the Breaking of the Seventh Seal or the Recreation of the Firmament.

It is so unexpected when she blinks that it scares off both the snake that stalks it and the forest wren. Slapping hand to hip as if to say There's nothing to be said, straight she marches across the field, up the hill, and down to the creek's edge. Off go the shoes and into the stream drops one of those pulsating toes. For a second before she has determined to evalute the water, her face accepts a grin.

Dinner time my little Minnie Mouse, I call out. We stare at one another for a second at the kitchen door before she pushes past the obstacle I have attempted to become. At table she proclaims: I am going to California when I grow up. By the end of the stew I see her mind is on Hawaii, and by bedtime she is bound for the Orient. But who knows? She may still go to California on the principle of it or out of spite—being an American.

*

There are several possible explanations for the bafflingly bizarre behavior of my charge:

1 I speak first from my role as a Psychological Hack: One day my "daughter"—as I've come to be accustomed to call her out of my desire for propagation of the species and fears of death—taking her fingers on a tour of her physique reached a point where her thumb turned the tint of a raspberry tart. So startled the former virgin was that had she religion she'd have straight-way returned to it instead of propelling herself, as she must, to the well where—

upon espying the rivulet of rose-colored liquid about to leave her ankle for her toes—she forced her frightened feet to the creek into which she abruptly dropped. At that instant almost guilt swept across her pale cheeks and—a few hours later—moved her to dye that coarsely carved doll of her identity's extension Prussian red. A day or two after she found herself compelled to repeat these events from end to beginning in reverse, commencing—and here my archetypically flushed face shows its Jungian self—the ritual which everyday I witness as I sit upon the porch and write to you of what I cannot every hope to comprehend.

2   So the Symbolist spoke: One day my rosebud rose in astonished ecstasy as Minerva, dragged across her breasts, came to rest in the cross of thighs and trunk. Out from the caves of her immaculate condition came a trickle of water which in a wink was switched to a whine of woe for that which had been toyed with. Gradually she rose further still until she stood upon her feet to find herself at the well too deep in which to bathe what was befouled between them. Into the bushes she crept coming upon a stream where she sat. Suddenly each object came into focus as something of significance to hold in the hands and relish in the heart as nuns

do relics of religions: the wine, the well, the bushes, the baby of wood, the water in which she washed.

3   The Pragmatist says: It's clear my little dear stuck her dolly's leg into her cunt and bled until everything was red.

4   The Rapist: I dreamt all of the above and went into her room where I saw the vessel from which so much confusion had come that I had to stop.

Which type do you think describes the writers of these letters as he is and as he was? Choose one of the above.

*

There are always rumors and I believe…. Mrs. Velde does not. You stop spoiling that kid with all them kisses, she commands. She-he not like no Hanusse brat. She-he is going to be the forester in Kansas USA Los Angeles. And for the life of me I can't determine of whom she is speaking, since I've only the cat on my lap.

Surely she can't mean the one with whom I've obviously been philandering. Ford could sleep beneath a tree, even in it, but he couldn't, I am certain, saw it down, strip it of bark, cut it into quarters, and hack notches into the ends of each piece so that, by plastering it with pine pitch and mud, it might be linked at right angles with its other parts. Minnie could, would pull down every coco, gum, and yew in the province if she got it into her head. But the very thought that Minnie would accept a kiss—let alone kisses—from this puss (yes, I still love the puns), is an absurd an idea as a cat making love to a mouse.

So I laugh and Mrs. V snorts, ripping off her apron as if she were about to jump into the river and pull a drowning swimmer to its banks.

Mr, you're a silly man.

*

From the other room we hear the scraping of fingers (sounding more like a hand of thumbs) across the narrow bands of horsehide stretched taut. It's Minne attacking her guitar with the grace of a legion of back country loggers lumbering into town on a Saturday night. Of two things even an Hanussee can be certain: Minnie is neither prodigy nor child. But as I've said, I encourage her (by saying absolutely nothing), hoping beyond even the boundaries of the faith some put in miracles that she—swept up in melody (more likely imagined than realized)—might someday swoon into the arms of the human race. Like all true believers I have severe doubts.

Come here a minute, sweetheart, I call out. She plays for five minutes more at least before she enters, her device of torture dragging after.

Yes?

It's time for your lessons.

She sighs, resigned.

Today's lesson comes from your uncle Leon, I try to entice.

You mean my father.

I've never been to Kansas USA or Los Angeles...

I'm going to California, she retorts.

...But I *have* been in Vermont where I've seen something approximating forests and where there may be foresters, I suspect.

Your uncle Leon took me there and taught me how to ski and create an avalanche.

Yes, there are mountains in America—like our San Germino—but with names like Stowe and Snow where wealthy people go to show they can pay the prices of a leisure life.

In order to ski you have to buy the proper clothing: duckdown parka, waterproof gloves, powder-blue snow pants, a Norwegian knit toboggan hat. You need to rent—if you can't afford them—Nordica NR 970 boots, Salomon 737E bindings, RCA Super Competition DH skiis, Scott Olympic poles, Alpine "Targa" goggles. You must procure time from an instructor of skiing or rely on a knowledgable and willing friend to teach you the half-sitting position, the full sitting position the step turn, and how to pick yourself up. When you assume the half-sitting position and, once again, move your left ski forward until the left boot-toe is just a few inches ahead of its brother, and you lift the tip of the left ski a foot off the ground in a slightly circular motion, returning it to its place on the snow flat, you need the friend for a little reassurance, a squeeze of the shoulder or a pat on the ass. And when you regain your confidence enough to move the right foot in the same manner, and you fall on the latter of those parts, you need your take your hand in his to pull you up and out.

Now you will Cover Distance. To do this, you must place a pole one foot in front of each ski opposite the boot. Drop into a half-sitting position, keeping your head erect. Slowly shuffle forward, applying the poles as needed to balance yourself.

To go downhill first you must look for obstacles, then balance your position, dropping your hands to your thighs while holding the pole shafts back until the glide down starts. You will need your friend to place his fore-arms under the pits of your arms and pull you to a standing position again.

To stop or slow your speed, if you are up to yet an-other run, you have to know how to force the skis into a v position without allowing them to touch. To get up from a fall is easy: 1) Remove the pole straps from the wrist; 2) Bring the skiis into a parallel position, if necessary rolling onto your back so that both skis are in the air over your body at once; 3) Bend the knees to bring the skis under your trunk, grasp your poles together and point them uphill about a foot from your knees; 4) Push yourself up into a sitting position or onto your knees until you can stand.

Back in your room you may ask your friend to light the fire or depending upon your accommodations to turn up the heat. If he is a good enough friend, he may even offer to rub the soreness out of your neck, shoulders, back, buttocks. As he begins the massage, you should relax, abandoning yourself to the "world of sensate pleasures," particularly if he pulls you up into his chest and folds his arms around your gut.

But you do *not* need to call your girlfriend, as he has his, an hour later to insist that you and he are so damn bored you wish she would catch the next plane up.

*

That was not my first glimmer of the fact that he who we so awfully adored, euphemistically speaking, was a bit confused in the bed. It wasn't just that he couldn't accept his sexual desires, but that he couldn't accept the possibility that others might. It was one thing to be "queer," but quite another to be accepted as "one." Self-loathing is always easier for conformists like Leon than is being admitted into a societal minority with open arms and hairy chests. In short, it was not the sex to which Leon objected, but the fact that I had not.

And so you too were telephoned. And we had that lovely weekend at the lodge in Vermont. And Minnie, conceived, culminated in the many marriages of L to L and H to me and me to L and L to H and H to L and L to me. And we all lived happily ever after.

Except that each of us, having never experienced happiness before, misunderstood what it was. How miserable we were, being happy like that!

*

Cross the continents come the shrieks of your indignance straight into my eardrums. How dare I tell a teenage adoptee tall tales like that!? Morality is always on the tip of your tongue.

I only wish Minnie *would* harken to my chronicle of father, mother, uncle, aunt—though we'll never know for sure, will we, who each of us was. But midway in my fair tale Mrs. V tows the princess off to scullery, ostensibly to sweep away the table crumbs and scrub the dinner pots, but in reality, to shield her from the scum she's convinced I have become.

It's all Earle Stanley Gardner's fault! The tales Mrs. V's sister tells of life in the United States are easily transferable to the life of a reprobate who, as every Hanuseese knows, not only lived in that land of honeyed money but was brought by a madman back to a folk who had to lock him away to spare their throats. So it is a simple slip for one who sees me actively attempting to corrupt my kin to imagine I'm the Devil's midwife. V has almost convinced herself, for instance, that I was party to the death of her beloved brother—who, you will recall, was under the employment of Americans when he (accidently?) strangled himself.

It's serious, don't laugh! As I told you, Mrs. V is very much admired hereabouts. I may even be imprisoned and shall have to write you the rest of these epistles from the bed of our gaolhouse. I've never been in prison—in Hanusse—so I can't report on its conditions and the needs for reform and such; but I should imagine out gaol takes as its model a mix of Spanish dungeon and Turkish whorehouse. Not a pretty sight.

I don't blame Mrs. Velde really for what she may do or even for the harm she may have already done. She's bored simply, and being very clever underneath her peasant face, she's rediscovered that old alchemical formula for goosing up her daily life with the golden aura of adventure and fuss. It's not so different by far from what Leon did or what you and I long to. It's quite astonishing to witness the extremes to which each of us will go to avoid the radical boredom of everyday living and in living every day, the radical flux.

Even I, who against all human instincts and community restrictions, have sought out the isolation and boredom of it all, who have opened my arms and embraced the dark and who have stared for hours on end into the sun, even I have just begun to understand why it was necessary to assign a grade of F to the final essay of my Freshman Composition class—although I doubt that Miss Marker or whatever my graduate student teacher's name was ever came to understand why she had graded it as such. For Juvenal was mistaken: bread and circuses are not distinct desires but are the same thing for the mob and gaolers both. Food in the stomach feeds the brain or what we traditionally have called the heart, and the brain alone can put meat on the bones. So it is with each of our entanglements and separations with and from others of the race: there can be no real distinctions made between our goings and comings, our pushings and pullings. our desires and distastes, our loves and hates. All are part of the vast machinery of the universe, are different instants merely in the single act of breathing, in and out.

I don't mean to imply that it doesn't matter which action one takes. If one breathes in without letting anything out, he gets too much oxygen and faints; and quite obviously if he chooses not to breathe in he quickly suffocates. To compromise moreover, is to weaken the chest and lungs; muscles need to be used in order to properly function. No, you have to breathe out in other to breathe in. In order to love you have to have been held in the arms of hate; in order to desire you have to know what you can't tolerate.

Leon and Lizzie, however, wanted it to go all in one direction, for everyone to come to a decision quick; and you wanted everything to stay frozen in one spot, halfway between the saints and the chamberpot. I've always wanted both, which is is to say I simply wanted to go on living life.

*

I take Ford into my arms to convince me that I still have breath. And I believe that today he senses what I seek for when we've finished he doesn't try to squim off, but stays to ask: You receive a letter from my mother yet?

No, I haven't been completely honest with him; I haven't had the heart to tell him that his mother has blotted out the fact of his existence and will never send a father he has never met to bring him back. Not that we would go with Don, Joe, or Jock, or any of the plaid-panted, husky-voiced, beer-guzzling football and cheerleader enthusiasts with whom you've come in contact. Ford would leave him standing on the dock, could never embrace either the philosophy or waist of one of your eternal adolescents trained by society to keep track of stock quotations, ballgame scores, and the averages of yards and balls struck by bats.

So as usual there's nothing to be said. But still he remains, reassuring, his hand against the shoulder blade of my back. It's better as it is.

I'm so appreciative I flush.

As you must know, however, I wouldn't always have agreed with that. One day I waited for you outside

Leon's studio for four hours before I realized that you'd missed the appointment you'd made to be "boned," "balled," "poked," "pounded," flayed," "screwed," "diddled"—or should we just say "fucked"? You'd have come to "copulate" or to "sleep with" him. You could never use a common name for anything you were doing or had done. Waltzing around the issue, that was how Leon described how you spoke. An interesting idiom that—dancing slowly round a concrete action you desire to abstract. I see Roseland—isn't that the name of the big New York dance hall?—with its silver-haired terpsichoreans gliding gracefully in circles near the walls. And in the very center of the room, equidistant from the four machine-cut columns which pretend to hold the ceiling up, a solitary madman swaying to the Tango or the Twist or the Bunny Hop.

When I finally figured out that you weren't going to come, I went inside to serve in your stead. By that time Leon didn't care much, as long as he could imagine that you and I didn't know he was "seeing" us both. So everything was hunky-dory since we knew and he didn't and Liz was almost always out of the house. For suddenly that year—for maybe two more, three at the most—everyone was Helen and Adonis, and that was what youth was about. It wasn't the sex so much—

certainly not that fleeting orgasmic flash—but the fact of the sex, the act of using the body while it was still firm! trim! and glistening white, black. As long as we were honest—a concept we confused with dropping our pants—we could do anything! go anywhere, bite off a corner of the Tower of Pisa and bring down the temples of a corrupt civilization with karate chops.

Yet we were frail and timid for all that. Because it didn't matter really that you missed your tête-à-tête and stayed home impatiently to wait. I couldn't love you more for being what you Americans call "a faithful wife," and you couldn't have been one anyway for more than a night. I couldn't care that you were cooking a turkey or basting a roast, not because your not being there gave me the opportunity to get a good—and it *was* a good—fuck, but because what really mattered and would matter still if I turned around at this very instant to find you watching me write, was simply that I should see you go safely into his arms and back into mine or off to your Don's, Joe's, Jock's. It's not just that I'm a voyeur. I needed to observe, to watch you on your way to wherever you went because I couldn't bear the thought that from wherever you went you might never be able to get back.

So when I came home to find you chaste for the day, laboring to become some kind of mate you swore to be in that silly ceremony blessed by church and state, I cursed you, of course! and stormed out of the conjugal paradise you'd cooked up for the night. To you— to everyone in shouting distance I am sure—love sounded like hate.

*

I shiver, call Ford back to me, and hug him close, afraid. The palmettos shiver with me in the breeze, but the too warm wind that shakes their leaves, lulls me back into my private paradise again. Do you suppose we all are drugged? That perhaps the Air Force sprayed the entire nation with some sleep-inducing mist back in 1970 or '71, a drug that seeps so slowly into systems that no one will know what hit him or her until one morning a decade or two away only the selected few will awake.

There are always rumors—yes, you accused me of living on the edge of hysteria, for believing every theory of conspiracy that the media relayed. But wasn't that what history taught us by 1968? That no matter how wild the imagination, no matter how apparently ridiculous the claim, the CIA, FBI, Office of the President, or obscure bureau of the government was cooking up a *pot au feu* that when it boiled over would brand the paranoid as a foolish old optimist. Even if *they* hadn't killed Kennedy or King *they* still could kill a brother, a best friend. When you heard the news, you erased George's name from your journal; I cursed the coffin when it arrived two weeks late.

*

Ford struggles to be free from my embrace. I teasingly wrestle with him so he may escape, he pinning my arm to back, I crying uncle to his laughs. Home again home again, however, Minnie stops me in my tracks. As I watch her helping V sweep away the kitchen spiders and swing the broom at our rafter-dwelling bats, my throat becomes brittle, the hair on my knuckles stands on end. Then just as suddenly these feelings pass. Just a little girl in front of me now playing African Queen, a naif imitation of Mrs. V's Buddha-like stature and stance. How embarrassing! I must be madder than I had imagined myself. For at that moment I swear I saw Satan—not a metaphor of him, not sign or symbol, or a little oaf with a lot of devil inside her breast. No. It was the Angel in Black, the baneful Beelzebub, the sour-smelling beast of perdition Himself.

The ancients would have stoned her on the spot. I pat her shoulder as I pass. I am not a madman. I am a socially responsible adult. These are not the days of hate, but of doubt.

*

Back in the olden days, if you recall, none of us was very good at doubt. We believed in everything—in racial equality, in social order, in peace and harmony and the eternal brotherhood of man—which is why everything so thoroughly came down on us like that. If only we'd focused on one or another of the worthy causes of the day. But we wanted it all, last night. Pamphlets on the evils of the Pentagon to the purchase of non-union grapes where shoved into hands that might have held their ears from our harangues on the immolation of the monks in Boa Ha and Bangkok. The energy of us!

It was inevitable. The cracks in a nuclear reactor are sometimes so fine that even a microscopic examination cannot detect them. Yet we have learned that what leaks through may destroy the populations of entire countries and states. But we went on believing in believing that as a group we were impervious to the emotional stew that brewed within each of our heads, hearts.

Did you ever see that great anti-conformist movie of the '50s, *The Invasion of the Body Snatchers*? We were a lot like the pods in that, with the ability to recreate ourselves into a kind of generic version of the individual—which, of course, was far better and bigger than any of us knew ourselves alone could become. That's the power that people living outside communes, clans, and intense families can never understand. Even a fool can become wise if in the eyes of his friends he reads that they need wisdom so badly they're willing to confer it upon him. Perhaps that is what wisdom always has been.

We were brilliant in any event. Everyone envied us— our insatiable search for truth, our beauty, our lusts. Even we envied us. And that, my love, is what is called a crack, a very fine-lined crack Leon alone detected. And that gave him power over us. For he knew what is known by every born leader, that in some tribes the chief controls his warriors absolutely by awarding them all battles before they are fought.

Such a one, however, pays a terrible price. For he alone must do battle with all that might arouse the tribe— their ideals, fears, desires. Such is the plague of the Christian God, to take all evil into oneself and transfer it safely into the space about. Christ could still forgive those who forced him to suffer; Satan could not.

Yet Leon wasn't evil in his hate, just stupid, confused, selfish, hurt. For I have seen evil.

*   *

*

From where does such a vision emanate?

How do those genetic memory chips of ancient cultural taboo transform themselves into the images cast by our minds into space? Are such visages products of a sort of psychodrama performed by the imagination upon the nerves linking cornea to brain? a kind of mass hysterical hallucination triggered not by the shared values of one's peers but by some neanderthals who sat at the mouth of a prehistoric cave? How horrible must have been that ancient apparition to have etched itself not in memory only but in chromosome!

In *The Structure of Destruction* Claude Ricochet, as always seeking "a history for what lies outside of it," describes evil as "a vision of our species before its capacity to fear and loathe what it would become." I find this intriguing, the idea that in order to come into consciousness man must have had to define himself "against what (s)he imagined s(he) unconsciously had been, done." Had she, like the tyger, torn at the throat of her territorial combatant? Had he too thumped chest, jumped upon the hinds of a passing member of his kind? At first it all must have seemed natural enough—until she saw perhaps another of her species leap upon the wholly mammoth, at water's edge he reflected on the bear behind him. Thing next to thing, "being beside being," as Ricochet describes it, awoke them to what they were not.

Over many a millenium (wo)man came to see theirself as a "not thing": I am not that—moon, snake, grass. I am no man, as Odysseus reveals himself to Cyclops. But the Greeks, as we know—as the Assyrians, Egyptians, and Hebrews before them—were tricksters who had already come to understand what they were not and sought to find out what they were in relation to the moon, snake—recently the grass, having drowned in the ocean, had become the hair of Poseidan's head, there to entangle the unwary traveler tacking his way through the scale of fish.

The gods above (con)fused themselves still, as ancients had, with horse, doe, dog, swan. A few mortals such as Acteon and Leda got a peek at that prehistoric past, and occasionally a shephard sacrificed a sheep to the good old days, but in general the human beast become an elitist as soon as s(he) comprehended his/her position.

Noah, proclaims Ricochet, was spared the flood not because he was morally superior to other men, but because—as our bibliographer—he achieved his God-given task to "lasso and list" all that he wasn't, the success of which made him a good "man."

The myth of the Flood, accordingly, is seen as a "history of the Expulsion from Paradise, to which the myth of Adam and Eve serves as emblem: There is the Eve who holds the tail of a python wound round the Adam delirious in its embrace. Uncoiling the serpent from about the man and pulling it out of the woman's grasp, Noah stuffs it into a box and carries it off to his craft. It rains a lot. A new creature is borne waving away from what (s)he was."

In short, evil isn't a condition, but is a position, a positing of one beside its brother. Around, away, on, above—these spiral about the dark unknown roots of being as surely as the ivy about the ivory columns of a masoleum. Evil is "a relationship of our present to a time without presence that we carry with us like tits and cock."

*

But what does it help me to know all that? As Ricochet admits, "The seeker of truth and its possessor is the difference between the philosopher and the common man." Minnie, for instance, is certain of her birth—that she is the daughter of Lizzie and Leon. And I believe she is right. But still I doubt. God, as punishment, could have slipped my genes into this manifestation of all I shun as a terrible tool of humiliation, a perpetual rebuke: Clay, you are not what you imagine yourself!

And her mother might possibly have been you, and Ford Lizzie's son. I should imagine that when the two of you gave birth so far away from the rest of us—if it was as simultaneous as you reported—that you couldn't stop that self-made midwife, Peter the Great Masturbater, from laying them side by side, and in so doing, mixing them up before he or either of you could have had time to attend to sexual organs and such. And if "my" daughter is yours, hers my son, both could have been fathered by practically anyone.

*   *
*

We take another walk. Or should I say I walk? For Ford speeds ahead without touching ground. Minnie drags behind playing her foot across the dust. It is painful to be between them. I do not have the stamina to catch up with what lies before me nor the patience to return to what we have passed. So I simply walk, desirous, of course, of what's before my eyes, guilty, as always, about what's at my back.

The light is lower now, slow as the sun begins to descend, hot. Minnie has come at the bottom of Scotch Hill to a total stop. Halfway up I too come nearly to a stand, so sluggish are my legs, arms limp. But I cannot let up. I become a snail leaving a little white trail where my boots lay the rushes against the chalk.

Minnie calls Come back. I wave her forward without turning to look: I don't want to see the anger burning into her soul as hate. But it is getting late, and I know as I reach the rise that her cry must cross my lips as I wipe the sweat from my face.

Soon as the salt dissolves in the lachryma of the eyes they witness what momentarily takes the brain aback—a plage as vast as a vision can swallow—that starting from the fall of Scotch spreads to the sea, more than 100 kilometers away. Empty. All empty. White.

Except to the right of the rise where a forest of Lebanon pines blots out all light underlining the sandy meadow in black. And it is this contrast, the chalk beach of white light pulsing against what appears from afar as a giant black hole in its space that catches the breath. And again catches it! For at that very instant my son, crossing plage to forest, disappeares from the horizon into the stand.

COME OUT OF THERE!

*

COME OUT OF THERE! GET OUT OF THE WATER you cried. As if Leon were likely to pay attention to Lizzie and you midway such an event.

74

You're not supposed to swim she scolded.

Swimmer that I was I still couldn't keep astride of Leon's reach, the pull of those bronzed biceps. But it wasn't that kind of match: it was more like a test, one of a series of tests to which each of us recently had been subjected. Will you ignore the posting? Will you follow me into the ocean? Will you pass through this sewage and oily scum?

Come back, you stamped.

The two of you had failed already—for the third time in fact. Refused to cross the line of teargas-tossers who blocked our march against the murderers of Kent. Refused to let yourselves be dragged down the concrete corriders of the Flushing Center for Induction. Refused to swallow the pills that promised a paradise of expanding minds acquired through Mickey the Nark.

Leon was desperate. So it didn't matter really if I lost. I had gone along with him. Like getting on a trolley or a bus in a strange city without the slightest idea of where and when it's going to stop. How far could he take us? A leader in doubt. A true leader doesn't take anyone— they follow because they must.

Leon took us everywhere. It was or wasn't fun. And he knew—or felt—or feared if he wasn't yet able to admit it that that passivity upon which he had propped up the entire apparatus of our coesion could at any instant snap. Which put him further into jeopardy than he had ever before been. Facing the cannons of the National Guard cranked down to his crotch he had cried Shoot then! And the city burst into applause. What he hadn't taken into account is that age-old separation between city and state, between the whole and habitat. Now it suddenly must have seemed as if everyone was headed back home to sing along with Lawrence Welk.

He didn't know, we didn't suspect that both of you now had expectations of another nature. But I don't think it would have mattered really had he known you were about to bear. For he, having too long lain in the cradle of your attentions had become the beast demanding it. There was no room for anyone else.

One gets tired. I turned over into a float. He turned to look over his shoulder halfway into a stroke and shuddered—I imagine—for the future he saw in my gut: a pot of fat. For he stuttered, wheezed, suddenly coughed, having swallowed, it appeared, some of the gunk.

Imagine me swimming out to bring him back.

Come back! I laugh. And I turn now into that future to look back down to where Minnie a moment before sat. She has vanished. And suddenly I truly doubt the condition of my head. Have I mislaid all facts, forgotten a future which has fulfilled itself long before I crossed its path? I blink. And still no sign of little sister. I shiver. Look back to the forest which swallowed my son. I am alone on the hilltop.

*   *
*

If she had a history perhaps! Might she return to the living? Cast off the spell of the reality I can't yet pronounce?

But what kind of history could that have been? I think of her mother, of telling her tale—metaphorically of course, for truth is always too full of color.

Genetics, moreover, is such an uncertain science based as it is on fruitflies and shrubs. We all know children born to evil folk—whose parents were equally evil and theirs before that—who are incredibly good. And similarly, the sweet old couple down the street have suddenly borne a sinful brat.

When I lived in New York I once visited a friend who with his wife lived in a most filthy flat. Papers upon everything interleaved with sandwich meats, coffee-stained briefs and panties, human hair, and years of dust. What furniture still stood was strewn about as if a convention of wrestlers had erupted from the spot upon my knock.

Samuel, their son, was not yet two years old, still stuttering in that tongue uninterpretable by adults. He liked me, we got on. He warmed my lap.

In search of cup and coffee pot the couple left the room. And immediately he slipped to the floor, waddled over to an upturned chair and righted it. Then on to another one, and another until—when the father returned his son retreated to the corner of the couch playing with what at his age we can still properly refer to as himself.

Sugar sent the father once more into the kitchen, and the son resumed his activities, dropping to his hands and knees, pulling, pushing, and uplifting every chair and table, or if they had not yet had the opportunity to fall, placing them along the plane of the wall.

Then, picking out a sandbox shovel from a burial of toys beside the couch, he attempted to brush the debris from what one supposed was once the rug.

Now what else could I have imagined but that the immaculate boy had grandparents living in some Park Avenue apartment, an orderly world ruled by unrelenting servants against whom my friends were taking psychological revenge.

On another occasion, however, I was invited to the father's family home at 110th Street; and on yet another visit I supped in the Bowery with the mother's folk. Each instance startled me more than the one before. By the time I'd been trundled round to scores of paternal and maternal uncles and aunts I had come to the conclusion that my friends were the issue of the two most filthy families in that foul-smelling, vermin-ridden, garbage dump New York. Our friendship faded at the flat of his great-grandparents in the Bronx.

Sows would have sought escape from such an estate. Rubbish covered all, and so having no place to sit we stood sipping at rum served up in bottles in which traces of jams and other somewhat jellied substances were caught beneath the lips. So we circled, like a herd of bison about to be attacked, round the patriach, propped-up on a pillow on the floor at our feet. In front of him sat three such glasses. One with an ochreous mixture of what looked to be whiskey and milk. Into the second glass went the ashes of what he called his "Conestoga" cigar. The third was empty until he bent and cast his spittle into it.

Suddenly from the corner of my eye I glimpsed the card table set—if you can call throwing plates and silver randomly upon its surface a "setting"—as our dining place. But what captured my attention was not the chaos of the table top, but the quick and rapid stalking of the same by a giant Norway rat.

I put down my glass and ran out into the waste of the gutter to vomit the potential dinner up. As I turned to walk away I saw a figure at the window. Perhaps it was the moisture of the night-dew that ran cross its grime, for the pane now appeared as a series of bars, behind which stood the fastiduous son who I now realize, at the early age of two, had already come to know the meaning of disgrace.

Again there is that possibility that in the nursery they got the babies mixed. The Levin kid got confused with the Spencer one. Perhaps the clean-living Levins as we speak have a dervish of defilement in their house. But as always I doubt. I have seen this too many times: the beautiful babe on the lap of the dour and disgusted bitch, the toad at the Madonna's teat.

The psychologists claim behavior. But can a child of one, two, even three be expected to have been conditioned, subconsciously as it would have had to have been, to reverse so many generations? I know what the psychologist will report: that the child will not necessarily perpetuate that pattern. He is merely searching for a self-identity that understandably is in opposition to the lifestyle of those around him. That this will pass; later, when he has reintegrated his newfound self within the community of family, schools, church— if there be one—and, yes, nation, he will quite likely fall back upon the patterns inbred within him through genes and played out by his parents in their activities of everyday life. In college, perhaps when he marries, he shall find himself ignoring the unmade bed, resisting the urge to upright that chair that fell as he stood upon hearing the news of his father's death.

But little Samuel never had a chance. While attempting to correct the position of his father's secretary, he tipped it into the direction of his unprotected temple, pinning himself into a conclusion from which he never awoke.

I, on the other hand, never stop sweeping sweeping the filth of my father out of my house. Of course I live in Hanusse, and my father doubtlessly was not a genetic pater. Perhaps I too am the son of some Spencer, who one estactic afternoon lay anchored in our enchanted bay.

*

I speak hyperbolically, however. For my father was not really a filthy man—just crude. Chuckling over every fart, grinning at all our toilet groans, he felt fulfillment in forcing his fingers into every bodily orifice that could entertain them. How he enjoyed our nightly pissfights! Keeps the body in good shape! Vinegars the skin, sweetens the muscle up. Like "champ-pain" (a verbal confusion, evidently, of what once a sailor offered and what my father took)—like "champ-pain" with a little bit of orange juice squeezed in.

I didn't mind. I didn't know any better. As if better had anything ever to do with knowledge—or history even. Like a long sick uncle who suddenly cries out in the night, I give up, better is a relative always—an explanation for what you and your neighbor do or have or don't do and had as compared with what you and he now do and have or did do and had before.

Are you better now? Improved somehow? Better off? I am not. I'm here and I'm always here and everything remains.

*

THE CASE OF THE INVISIBLE BIRTH

Once there was a woman who gave birth to an invisible child, a newborn visible to others but not, evidently, to the woman from whose womb it had come.

The labor was long and hard as labor generally is, and painful in a way no general laborer can comprehend. And when the child had been finally brought to light and properly beaten, the mother, utterly done, fell into a sleep so deep that anyone but a reassuring physician might have the called the coroner.

But she awoke, as the doctor predicted. And the babe was brought directly into the bedroom and laid beside.

She looked down to where the woman had seemed to deposit a package, blinked, and cried Where is my daughter, my son?

Beside you ma'm. There—the nurse needled its neck— There now. Don't fuss.

The eyes of the mother had followed this action but could not determine their source.

Where is my baby? Are you deaf?

No ma'm. I hear you fine. But you're still whoozy a bit. The baby lays beside you asleep in the bed.

Again the eyes followed the course of her body's line, but nothing they witnessed seemed to satisfy them. Where?

Pursing her lips, the nurse grabbed thin air, spun to the door, and whipped out.

Later that day the doctor came by. Dear, dear me. How is the old system. You've gone through a long one. Very tough.

I presume you're paid by the hour?

Right to the heart, right to medicine's heart. I know your kind. We've lots of you critics. And when you come to us, still we put everything back into place.

For ten hours of torture you can't claim that! And I'd choose it again over your cut and paste. But I lived! Now bring the babe who at the end of my sentence stuck in the question.

Always ungrateful. After all of our study, a study that takes more time than any ten women to carry, to learn how to alieviate the curse. Like a camel coming out of an ass, that's how they taught us to imagine it. I have hemorrhoids. Not so hard really to understand that it is truly something that hurts. So I figure what's a little ether but gold in the purse.

The body knows when and how to collapse. The mind can take just so much. My lawyer will be in touch.

Enter the nurse, cautiously, smiling. Your baby. What you gonna call him?

Her, the doctor interjects.

Her? The eyes plead at the impossibility of what they can't comprehend. Why are you doing this?

What ma'm?

That is what I mean. You need rest. More rest.

Don't you come near me!

The bottle goes back into the pocket of his waistcoat. Hold your baby then.

She hides her hysteria. At the crook of her arm, she observes the nurse about the enter into ecstasy at the sight of child and madonna. Get out of here she growls through her teeth.

The nurse bends to collect the invisible infant.

Out of here! Now!

But—

Out!

So the nurse leaves the mother alone with that which she still cannot conceive. The mother strokes the bed-spread, the sheet, the slip of bedshirt that covers her hips, puts her lips the the mattress and howls.

The father, called by the doctor to come and confirm that this woman, his wife, is suffering under delusions, is overwhelmed by the sight of his progeny. Oh, she's beautiful. Beautiful Marie!

Marie?

Her name, if it was a girl, we agreed.

What name? And what do you see to put such a simple sound to it?

Don't you remember, my love?

She is more confused yet. Minerva, after my aunt.

Minerva? You call Marie a coarse thing?

Minerva, the Goddess of Invention.

She gazes at her side, importing him. Where?

He, appalled, pets the child. She was nothing but a whimper left.

So when the house was still she kissed the air beside where her body lay. And in that act of dreamy conjugation it turned into a lie, and grew and grew into my Minerva, my Minnie, into you.

*   *
*

You. A concept unthinkable in Hanusse. For to recognize "you," one must have an "I." One must see one's self different from the name applied, imagine, at least, that a Minnie could be a Betty, a Grace, even a Paul. And that that Paul might be completely silent, the Grace able to move across this still room in accordance with her name, the Betty ready to sit beside forever with a simple smile upon her lovely face. There is Minnie, plodding now directly through the patch of sun as if it were burning grass desperate for her stomp and stamp. Minnie on the march, unable to conceive that within there could be another lithe and delicate someone. For Minnie, however, no one else exists, without or within. Other folk—Ford and I—are just things in space with more or less reality than the grass she lays flat, the stove she kicks, or the bonnet she has now strapped to her back. We are different only because we talk, because we do not sit as Betty, Grace, and Paul in an eternal triangle of peace. We kick back. So we've become a field of nettles, a habitat she would prefer never to encounter again. But there are berries on these bushes, and one (the one named Minnie) has to eat.

Minnie, accordingly, cannot conceive a history. For history, we recognize, not only has a self to repeat, but a self from which, potentially at least, it can deviate. Why else depose a despot, elect a president, bow before a king? The rise and fall of entire nations is dependent upon the recognition of "you" and "me."

Yes Hanusse, as I've said, has no past. In that sense we are free, free to be stupidly what each of us is. Perhaps I am Paul, sitting in that silent room with Grace and Betty by my side, and cannot comprehend the fact. Instead I sit here on a hilltop in the bright sun to write.

But I do not question it. Unlike Leon I do not try to imagine and control the future course of our lives.

For the truth is apparent now that, although we lived (or were reported to have lived), we had no lives, no life each. We were determined to become what we had determined was worth determining. If, as some psychologists insist, the human race is not more than a very large colony of rats, then might it not be preferable (so we reasoned, you'll recall) to run down the maze after cake or candy or creamy chocolates instead of cheese? If the path is predictable, the reward could be, should be for those who could imagine it as such, something different, a treat. So we ran, very cleverly at that, demanding all along the way that we get justice, that instead of cheese we be served chocolate cake. But when we reached the last bend we could see way up ahead—there were no chocolates, no candies, cakes, nor even cheese. For this time it had been a test just to see if we, as rats, would run with nothing—no smells to lead us on—save hope and racial memory of something being at the end. You were too hungry to go back. Leon was too proud. And Liz, as we know, had got lost along the way. Only I was able to return to where I had begun.

Come back, I call out. Come back.

90

And so, we had no histories, in fact. Just a good run for the money, so to speak. It might have been different I suppose if the Gods (those lab technicians hovering over us so high) had decided to try, as an enticement, some sweet crumbs. In the end, I suppose, we would have settled even for the cheese, like Minnie sitting down to berries in the nettle patch.

Here she is, coming back. I hold out a chocolate in my left hand. How she hates when I do that! But she takes it, rips away the foil, throws it into her mouth, and chomps.

A good bite, my little mouse. No cheese for you. No run through the maze. No blind turns, ramps. Those who have never left have no need to be called back.

I should have called out to Ford, *Don't go*! But I know it would have made no difference.

The sun has gone under clouds and what was black has not become a verdant celebration: grey-greens against pea, patches of yellow green in the midst of forest, ripe young buds of emerald waving cross dark evergreens and white-tinged moss.

Minnie and I turn back to the house, she suddenly
sullen now since she has finally reached a destination,
I, tired somehow, tired of trying to tell you what you
are missing, and in a moment of exhaustion, turn to
Minnie to make it up, putting an arm around her neck.
It is a gesture, an encouragement for the two of us to
sing our little marching jingle:

> Marching to perdition
> we are in condition
> to get to the position
> of our knees [together we collapse].
> Pleasssse—help us kick up
> a ruckus, Jesus, lift up our tuchis
> and we will march march march
> (what the Hell!) straight
> to Heaven after all.

*   *

*

I have only now been able to obtain more paper. So
another year has passed—according to our "calendar,"
which takes up a third of the wall of what we call our
kitchen. Every day V draws another circle on our wall
rising and crosses it with an x upon going to bed. When

she has marked some thirty such circled x's she draws the circle but does not enter anything within. Then back to circled x's once again. When she has reached some 350 of such circles—I am not certain she counts *all* the circles or only the circles with the x's in them or even if she *can* count—she draws the circle upon the floor and darkens it with her presence. And we, rubbing our bodies with coal and in complete undress (she has left on her "necessities"), draw her away from the center into our little circle formed by holding hands. We dance and dance, faster and faster, until the first to collapse is put in the center, round which we close tighter and tighter until it is only two (usually Ford and me) who surround, moving closer and closer in until the others unfairly begin to tickle and try to trip the dancers up. Ultimately, they fall also: the circle now filled with wiggling black bodies.

And we go back to whatever it is we will do. Nothing much different from the year just passed. I am here every year. The hurricanes have come again and gone away, followed by their floods and the floods of tourists and a new generation of Hanussee after that. I have retreated and returned. The children had been satisfied and have again become desperate. Mrs. V is desperately dissatisfied, telling our neighbors I am not a normal man, having read another detective tale. And to me it *is* a mystery, how we passed so suddenly from twelve whites to black.

You—in my imagination—have traveled to Morocco or to the Sudan. Beware the desert dear! They'll bugger you like some boy if you don't join the harem. Of course you'd go along with that—joining the harem, I mean. You'd think it might *save* you somehow—see it sort of like becoming a nun—or a saint even, being caught up in something so much bigger than yourself. I don't mean that dominating organ, but the *system* which serves and celebrates itself even more than the sheik. Must be a little like living in a nunnery—a salacious one. So many women all dressed up and nowhere to go. I wonder what the incidence of Lesbianism is.

Enough! I know you're not in the Sudan. I have that much hold of reality yet! Minnie creeps to me. Yes, I'm writing your mother, I admit. So what?

I have learned, she says, how to make a letter and someday I shall mail it.

I am flabbergasted! Where did you learn that?

94

I copied it from Mrs. Velde's book.

What letter?

A letter.

The letter A?

A letter. I'm going to mail it. And she will come for me and love me as a mother must!

Suddenly she is in tears. But before I can call come here, she runs.

I sit for a moment, pondering what just occurred. Has she actually copied out an entire letter from Perry Mason or—and I realize this has to be it—has V somehow spitefully taught her the first (and only letter that she knows) of the alphabet? I can see her letter to you now:

A

A gift. Something she imagines you can—must—appreciate, celebrate even. As she sees me here, year after year, writing, writing, she can only imagine—knowing that you never have answered me—that *one* letter, her letter may achieve what thousands have not. Yes, that has to be it! A single letter. For when I said that Mrs. Velde reads mysteries, I did not mean to imply that she knows *how* to read. The local scribe *retells* her the tales, which she, in turn, tells to her friends—and back to herself eventually—turning the pages of the books as she speaks. It *is* a reading of sorts, but how different from what we learned at the university. Let us call it a *sympathetic* reading. She remembers the details, sometimes even the plot. She does not really understand the *meaning* of it. It is like someone who can recite the story of a movie, scene by scene, image by image, but has never witnessed one.

Yes, it is A, the letter A. It has to be! The scribe must have pointed out an A to V. *A* moment later, for example. *A* lady of great wealth.

A moment later, a woman of great wealth enters the room: it is Minnie holding her letter A upon a pillow heavily brocaded by an Arab harem. She puts the pillow upon her bed and curls up with head against the letter imagining all the messages she might send. *A* letter. Her alpha.

Your end.

She shall learn no others! I swear it! Although she now fetishizes one word, I will prevent her from discovering others. Fortunately she does not comprehend it as an article, even though she does recognize as a *thing!*

O Minnie, how can I explain? *A* moment is *nothing*. A woman of great wealth is a person who can purchase almost anything she wants but the song you are now attempting, a least, to sing.

> Dominick nick nick nick nick
> Dominie nay nay nay nay
> We all from time to time will stray.
> Dominick nick nick nick nick
> Dominie nay nay nay nay
> And some will get away!

*   *

*

I taught her that, obviously. I couldn't remember the real lyrics. I didn't even understand the song when I first heard it. What year was that? The signing nun! Tell your children about that one! On the program tonight Janis Joplin will spill her guts which the singing nun will clean up! And they were on the same *programme*, standing for what's right and what's worth living for: real honesty and peace.

What we never understood was that between the two there was a war—not the Viet Nam war—but a war between whatever the fuck the singing nun was promoting and the sounds Janis Joplin cracked out. Another crack, a crack in our ideals. The Catholics didn't want intestines on their stage.

Unless they made the cut.

Way back then we were in a kind of haze, a haze that prevented us from—heirloom of our stupidity—the impending world of cynicism and doubt. We were desperate to embrace. Like an army of blindly stumbling whores we put our arms about everything in sight—from human bodies to imprisoned park benches, from the fuzziest of concepts to the Prolegomenon of Kant. And so we hugged to our bosoms good and evil both. Did it matter which was which? Was there a difference?

Of course there was! But who shall determine that? Many will try, for that is what power is all about—and why our assinine assurances of love stopped (temporarily) entire governments in their tracks. For it is differences that make, so to speak, all the difference, the belief that one belief is to be believed over another one. I am not speaking of mere spirituality; those men in labcoats prodding their mice believe they have the right to prod the mice; the mob believes the intellect is a dangerous rat; the whiz kid wires a system to protect the banker from the mob; the banker believes it is practical to keep the investor from his assets; the investor feels the need to take the manager's hand from his pocket; the manager shall steal the words from the worker's mouths; and the worker—when he is not the mob—cannot resist restraining the vermin entering the maze of his daily race. Power is difference; it has nothing all to do with class. As Ricochet writes, Cain could not be Abel. Even the difference the mirror reveals between concept and construct can lead to discomfort.

Another crack! So gargle every night and—when you see yourself in the aging mirror—laugh. Or you too can be caught up in that contagion of cataclysmal catechisms. Thou shalt do this, shalt not do that. For love breeds hate in the hearts of some, and hate breeds love in others; but whether it's hate or love there's a power in people who believe in believing one or the other. And both suck the breath away until you lay on top or on bottom in a gasp.

The Hanussee, as I have said, are not believers: we leave the tourists to believe for us, since we are such unsure folk. Lady, want a photograph?

*   *
*

The climate is cooler or warmer by just a degree or two than it was the year before. So we still sweat flies and swat the perspiration from our foreheads out on the little veranda where we gather, just before dark, to drink the concoction of sugar, water, and alcohol we call May Ties in honor of Minnie's mispronunciation. Minnie likes them, and slurps them up fast. Ford sips, and slips off before he finishes even one. They—drinks and children both—remind me of the time I was in Paris. (Oh, I know, I said I was never anywhere; but I have been there when I followed Leon). In a Paris restaurant you often sit very close to your fellow diner.

That can breed intimacy—or it can produce a kind of claustrophobic crick in the neck as you look away from the crevice of your nearest neighbor's mouth, be it with occupied language, food or cigarette. Once in Paris I sat next to a little bureaucratic monk, who, being, as I was, alone, said not a word. But he ate—well, a horse is a just exaggeration—of his gargantuan steak. He ate it with *pommes frites* and *salade* and several slices of good French bread. And he had desert after and café and cognac and another. But all very quick. And then he went away, and I got my appetite back and ordered a *petit faux en crab*. Another man came next to me and sat. This one was an English one, so I understood. For he looked exactly like the Frenchman who had just departed. But he ordered next to nothing, just a piece of cheese sliced. And at that he nibbled the edges merely. And then he finally went away. I would never eat at this restaurant again.

That is the point in my last epistle I was trying to make: There are some who would, if they could, swallow an entire universe, and still feel hungry. Others, if they might, would spit out even that air they have dared in their meager lives to suck into their sick lungs. Yet both have the same desire: to have attention paid. For normality is nothing more than trying to blend in. It leaves the sufferer silent. It is at the extremes—those at the edges—where the strong and weak or the mad and the meek hold sway. Get out of their way! Take a piece of my heart! Dominick nick nick nick nick!

Minnie has fallen to sleep. V carefully carries her in, depositing the burden on the nest of bamboo and palm leaves we have woven into what we call "the bed." V comes back for a final drink.

Scribble, scribble mister, don't make mother come.

No, it doesn't, I reply.

Why? Does mother *hate* daughter, *hate* son?

She's never seen them—except at birth. And even then…. I'm not certain.

Why?

Because some mad man couldn't bear the thought of losing them—their mothers.

What is this meaning?

102

I don't know. He thought *he* knew.

What? What did man know?

That he was the father.

Was man father?

I don't think so. Or he wasn't the only father.

Meaning?

I think *I* was the father.

Two women? Two babies?

Perhaps.

This is perverse.

I was a tourist.

Not here.

No. Not here.

It is time to take daughter.

Not yet.

It is time. Minnie grows. Early.

Not yet.

It is not right.

I know. Not here. Pretend.

Pretend?

I am a tourist.

Father is tourist. Father cannot be father again.

I don't want to be.

Nussia will take daughter.

Nussia?

Nussia, she says, bowing from the head. V has never before breathed her name.

104

Nussia. I like Nussia.

She grins, putting her fingers into the shape sailors must have once—as a teenager of course—forced her fingers into: V, for victory. Velde is our personal earth-bound designation of that residual teenage affectation. Suddenly she is beautiful: I can see through the harridan she has become to the Nussia, so vibrantly young.

Not yet.

Tomorrow.

Perhaps next month.

Tomorrow.

Next year.

Today.

And she is up and off. It is the Hanussee way: the further one bargains into the future the nearer the auctioneer draws the present back into fact. It is the same at market: You say 1,000, he says 50. You say 2,000, he says 5. Economists have a problem with that. Tourists delight in the bargain they think they have got.

Not yet. Come back! I stay alone on the veranda with the incessant cricketing of the night. We don't have fireflies. I remember being so amazed at their existence on one August evening. What *are* they I demanded to know?

What?

Those!

Fireflies, you scoffed. I'll get you one. And from the balcony where I stood transfixed, you suddenly alighted—via apartment door, elevator, and split-second timing—to capture one—a firefly, which—via elevator, door, and quick-time march across the living room back—you presented to me within palms cupped. It sat for a moment upon their opening, stunned by release, and, as if suddenly remembering itself, flew off. It was the most beautiful present you had given me, is still to this day the most wonderful gift I have ever received.

But we have crickets; we have stars. We have—ourselves. Which is something we did not have, in Leon's little club. My children—they can be Leon's, it makes no difference—have themselves, even if, as with Minnie, they don't know what that represents. I love them. Dearly. Beyond normality because that is where I have had to take them in order to love them so they could discover themselves—themselves without a sense of self, without a sense of *difference.*

Ford *is* his tree, Minnie, her doll Minerva, and soon, so it appears—if V. is to be believed—an adolescent, which is a dangerous transition here in Hanusse for the female species. Do I want her to muck around in the pants of some British Peter, French Paul, or American Dick? I hate her, I have to admit, in loving her so much. She *is* different. That is why the Hanussee retreat to what they know best: to eschew the difference, to accept themselves as sexual beings neither superior to nor lesser than what they are and were and will always be. Old age weds youth in a symphony of sympathy: man to man, woman to woman. The sport, in Western cultures, is to play out the power of the event, to control or pretend to or pretend not to but do, or do and really don't. We find that to be such an utter waste of time and energy. Why not take unto yourself that about which you know as much as you know about. But women, in our culture, must first walk the gauntlet, accept the "favors"—statement of power stronger than Atilla the Hun could even have known— of the stranger to engender an uncertain and insecure new being, welcome to us because it is as confused as we will always be. No father. Just a young, unwitting mother. I am nobody, no body. The irrefutable logic of it all.

In the middle of the night Ford curls to me, head upon my breast, his smooth little ass against my penis, quickly erect. We sleep that way, in comfort and ex- pectation of what dawn may bring. In the morning I am wet, not with sexual excitement and release but from mother nature herself. What is the difference?

In Hanusse, there is none, since we have no words in our language to separate the natural from nature, or nature from human nature. What is natural is human, what is human is natural, naturally. Ford has ejacu- lated all over the fronds in his sleep. Night emissions Leon told me they were called in his childhood (who could imagine a childhood for him?). Emissions, as if it were a burp, a piss. No. Even the adolescent sleeper knows this is something different, something so powerful that…his whole body shudders to the pleasure of his dreams. If you piss, you wake up wet, cold, relieved perhaps, but without a smile. A fart feels for an instant nice—nothing more, nothing less. No, ejaculation is not just an emission, but a projection upon the subconscious mind of what the conscious will find to be absolute bliss.

*   *

*

But enough of this! I am again at retreat, writing our lives and dancing my dance in this old hall where sailors came once to jig, jug and lug. Across the wooden floor, I swear, some evenings I can see little pools of their blood. That is the reputation of the place—as I have ever so gradually uncovered the facts; they came here not just for the alcohol but for the attendant brawl. So out of way this place was, I suppose, that they were safe from shore patrols. And living in such confined quarters for so many months must have created many resentments, hatreds, jealousies, and intense loves. One could pound the floor equally with feet, fists, head, so it appears, at the Hilltop Club.

Some died of injuries my mailman said, finally delivering up the gossip I had for years sought. One—one hung himself—in sorrow it was said for the blow deposited in his bunk mate's mouth in return for the many he had, more pleasurably perhaps, received throughout their voyages. His quite lit mate apparently had come to collect favors commensurate, and having been presented simultaneously with the physical blow and linguistic response, fell back (both literally and symbolically) to his former position of head to crotch upon a neighboring seaman who misunderstanding his desires or discontent thereof had as quickly come to the decision to heave way or sway with the wind of circumstance. In his hand moreover he held a woman's wrist whose fingernails had just begun to poke the vertebrae of his spine, stimulating him into a shiver that sent what at the opposite side was suddenly abulge directly down the stunned bloke's throat who—on account of beer, beating, and nerve and motor discoordination—heaved in the most literal sense of the word, in response to which his recent acquaintance determined—on account of beer and nerve and motor discoordination and disgust—heaved as well the head of what was soon to be a dead man to the floor where it split upon hitting it. The witness to all this, he who had hooked his gifthorse in the mouth, was later found strung up in the knot of his own rope over the urinal where many a sailor had got pissed and relieved themselves.

So this is the room where many a sailor was doomed, less by Circeian transformation than their their bestial backsliding. It is a perfect place—for me, for what I'm doing, for what I've done.

Not for what I've done to you, to Leon—even Lizzie— but for what I haven't done, didn't do: Leave you alone to die in peace. For that's what would have happened, I now know, had I not come along. The drugs alone would have killed you. You saw what it had already done to Liz. First the habits, the hours she spent brushing teeth; then eccentricities: one nail red, one green, three pink; finally the terrors—at the end she would not even leave the house. I remember one night—long before you could have been pregnant with Ford—you demanding for at least three hours that I get you pickles, pickles, all kinds of pickles: sour, salt-cured cucumbers, sweet wine laced gherkins, little green cornichons. Perhaps you were pregnant and had an abortion. Had he known Leon wouldn't have given you a choice. But I was stupid. As you see, I was stupid. Just now realizing that must have been the source of your obsession. Pickles! I must have pickles! Lots of pickles. I refused. Told you to calm down. Take a sedative. I would have known that that was my child— or at least interpreted it as such. Leon wouldn't have been able to claim Paul, Betty, or Grace.

Rouging your larynx is another matter! Madness was surely behind that. It's sexy, you insisted. It's stupid, I declared. Like a mole! It's sexy. Larynxes aren't moles unless they lie within the necks of spies, I retorted. Perhaps I am a spy, you teased.

You see, I remember all of that. By now I should have forgotten. Gotten over what I did find sexy in the end, because it was so silly, and you believed it or at least pretended to. The drugs were slowly changing us.

One day I couldn't remember where I put my car—or even if I had driven it (which of course I would have had to), or even if I had one. Or if I did have a car what it would look like, what color, what make. Or how to drive had I had one. Did I have a key? That was when I stopped. I didn't tell you. I didn't tell Leon or Lizzie. Not a soul. Perhaps you had stopped too. Suddenly you no longer roughed that dimple atop your cleavage. And I missed it—a bit.

Still, it was too late. Too late for you. Leon had control over what you thought and what you said. Let's go to moon, Leon commanded. Yes, said Lizzie. Let's do. Find me a way, you skeptically jested. But you'd have boarded, if he'd planted a rocket in front of your house. I don't blame you. Even I had second thoughts when I had him committed. Second thoughts when I knew he would have killed me, Minnie, Ford, anyone with whom he came in contact. Would have killed us—just as he killed Lizzie and you.

You see, I'm not really as insane as I seem. Writing letters to a dead woman—pretending she's in Spain when I know for a fact her bones have long since decomposed in a little damp cemetery on the outskirts of Madrid, Iowa, where there is one public and one obviously parochial school (Catholic because its ancestors came from the capitol of the country you never got a chance to visit.). You were never in Paris, I admit. The harem shall never see your face.

* *
*

Dear Hannah,

Come back! I need you—if only to finish this tale. Let me tell you a story you'll be sure not to like. Once upon a time a King, a very good king, wanted for his daughter, Princess Périgourdine, only the best. The best shoes, the best hat, the best dress. Now it was time for the best husband he could find. Who might he be? And where would he come from? There is never a consort in the court! Yet he was tired of *tests*—of watching young men carrying a princess to mountain tops, of their answering three riddles concocted by clever princesses, of their slaying all the dragons thereabouts. Tests were out of date, so old fashioned. Love was possible, but the Princess, well to say it as politely as one can, was plainly handsome. If the husband he found was to be the best, he had to make a dashing figure with a well-chiseled chin, hirsute and muscle in the arms and chest, a nice little tush, shapely strong legs with all of this planted on two perfectly thin arched feet. The King was very particular about feet. And about things too particular for us to pursue.

So the King decided to give interviews. The word was sent about: YOUNG MAN WANTED, MODEL, MUSCULAR, HIRSUTE WITH THIN, SOMEWHAT LONGISH SHOES. Now as you know, when such a call goes out the fat and squat and thick and round and red-faced, blue-nosed, droolers come along for the interviews as well. So the King was very busy for a long while and had nearly forgotten his wife. As the interviews reached their second, their third and fourth months without a son in sight, the Queen complained. Why do all these young men come to *you*?

Frankly, my dear, I'm frustrated! I didn't know my kingdom had so many toads. But if I want the best for my daughter, I must look under every rock.

I wish you'd crawl under one yourself, said the Queen, angrier than she had meant to be. I'm tired of being alone!

I have a duty to your daughter, don't I?

I'm going to my mother's for a while.

You're leaving me?

Don't you think that would be best?

Yes, I guess I do. Under the circumstances. If only I could find a Lancelot!

Not without a Guenevere, my dear, was the last sentence to him she spoke.

The daughter and dad stayed on, playing checkers or parcheesi or what ever kings and daughters do. And many the night it was he praised the qualities of the Prince for which he was on the prowl. At which times, she, the cherished child, habitually curled up her lip

115

in disdain and disgust. I'm never going to leave you daddy, she proclaimed.

At which times the King found her, to put it politely, not only plain but absolutely ugly. And what with toads by day and the pampered Princess every night, the King grew even more determined to bring beauty into his life.

Day after day, the drudgery. Name, Kingdom, please. Next. And for the few that were even somewhat passingly pleasant the request that, would they please undress? In their nakedness he inspected them for blotches, rashes, cuts, growths, scratches, blemishes, tattoos, warts, muscle distribution, pectoral development, inclination of the tummy, thinness of the hips, firmness of the ass, overall hairiness, length and width of penis, shapeliness of leg, arch of foot and the particulars into which we will not butt. It took him hours—and he was never entirely satisfied with the result. Not a few complained of such thorough inspection which, quite obviously, ruled them out from the start—or at the end if the complaint were delayed. The King came to realize that the process would be a long and arduous one; but since he was still young (you must remember Kings were often wedded in those days at the age of 10 or 11 or 12) and eager to find beauty, he carried on.

None of these young men, however, was absolutely perfect, worthy enough to place his head upon his daughter's breast (did she have one? he pondered) and other things in the netherparts (the thought brought a shudder to his head). Next. Name? Kingdom? Day after day. And so it went.

Now before I tell you the rest of the story, let me tell you another one, just a little one to allow the King time to discover the Prince you know he eventually must. There was a woman who was seeking a husband—not a prince but a nice decent man with whom she could be comfortable and by whom she could be stimulated—intellectually and sexually—and who might look good or even possibly be really handsome, and whom (it would be nice) had a good income so that they might put their children (three to be precise) through school and, since the university costs were rising every year, who had, perhaps, an excellent income and, since he would necessarily like a nice house to come home to, and, if it wasn't asking too much, could be rich and stunningly beautiful too, and, well it wouldn't hurt, would be romantic and advertursome, bringing her flowers and chocolates on his way home from Wall Street every night. Well, let me tell you, she found just the man. He was very rich.

Although he was a bit rounded in the cheeks—both at head and behind—he was, everyone told her so, really handsome and would be a beauty if he were just a bit taller and did something about his tummy—and the blood pressure which made his face red. And he was sort of dashing—as he dashed about between the office and the house twice a day, often late at night. And he was certainly adventursome, given the fact that he invested in Lipp and Lipp stocks from which lost his shirt, which, I can tell you, was not a pretty sight. But it was all right. The boy whom they adopted was not very bright and wound up in a reformatory school instead of a college.

One day the King called order to his court and heralded in the suitors to be. No one, so the page informed him, had arrived. May I be so brave sir, spoke the liege, to suggest that you have used nearly every man up.

I beg your pardon! thundered the normally good natured monarch.

I mean, sir, with my apologies for my mean way of expressing it, what I mean is that there is no one else.

Now the page had been in court from his boyhood, but for the first time the King recognized the child was now a full-fledged adolescent, 17, perhaps 18, 20.

Get undressed.

Yes sir, the page replied. And without hesitation, even for an eye's blink, he took off his doublet, blouse, and dropped his tights. The King rose, coming over to inspect at closer range. Blemishes there were none, muscular development—perfect. Pectoral same. Tight ass, thin hips, shapely legs. The feet were arched. Although it had not grown completely in yet, there was no doubt that the lad would be blessed with heavy hair on his ass and had already a good bush of black just above what was, oh, quite long, quite thick, quite now in a position at angles with a body so proportionately exact that the King could scarcely keep the awe from slipping through his lips, and so, as suddenly, sought to protect such a commonplace release by stuffing the member at odds with other angles of the boy down his throat. The boy's grunt of pleasure said it all for both.

Upon completing the tour of the young man's torso, the King drew back. You shall marry the Princess, he proclaimed!

I shall not, the lad spoke up!

The King, having never before been contradicted except by his wife, was a bit taken aback. Associating such audacity, accordingly, with spousal abuse and expectation, he countermanded: Then you shall marry me!

Gladly spoke the proud, future ruler, will I serve you as I always have. And so, just as you knew they had to, they lived forever happily. The Princess? She was the one I told you about. The one who sought and found a rich fiancee who lost it all and slit his throat. Consequently, she moved to Rheon where, after marrying the local postmaster there, she had a daughter who, if you recall, had a son without the usual male encounter. She too was blessed.

And *her* son? I don't want to spoil the plot.

*   *
*

Hannah, I have to admit. I do not feel the children are safe. Yes, I have nightmares still about Leon—a possible escape. But it isn't just that! I have had a vision again. Minnie was just sitting there, doing absolutely nothing, when huge wings sprouted from her shoulder blades. At first, I thought the vision pleasant. Perhaps, afterall, she was an angel... At that very second of perception, however, I sensed a slight irritation of my nose, and soon a horrible sulphurous smell arose. I almost passed out. Minnie still sat, at table I remember it, head bent over her doll, while smoke begin to swirl around her head and teeth replaced her smile—tea-stained, black and brown, tiny, little incisors and pointed yellow canines. It was not all of a sudden, but a gradual transformation, a slow descent into the Satanic state—until, too late, I realized she *was* Beelzebub. For I watched this not, at first, with fear, but with utter fascination, as inch by inch before my eyes she transmogrified into everything anyone who loves hates.

One vision I can take. Two! Am I on drugs? No! Have the drugs of the past permanently affected my head? I don't think so. You'll have to judge. I have no other correspondent—I mean, no one.

Minnie mocked me, spoke in several tongues. My first reaction—I still cannot believe it!—was the thought that I was hearing things. Guten abend, Herr Mayenne. Bonjour. Like Berlitz. You see such things in movies. Farvell—and as suddenly He disappeared. Minnie sat before me, a little confused I thought, but implacable as she is always. But then—then I knew something had happened between us: I feel strange, she said. I hurt. I'm afraid.

Minnie has seldom before admitted to any particular emotion, except if you want to apply such a term to hunger, tiredness, boredom.

Are you all right?

I'm afraid.

Yes. I should imagine, I said, more hesitantly than I wanted to speak. Come here, I said, as if in slow motion, fear in my own voice perhaps.

No! Don't hurt me!

No. I won't. Where does it hurt?

Here, she pointed at her shoulder blades, first left, then right. I have to throw up.

Out the door you go. I ushered her there—where, after her retch, I put my arms about my wretch, hugging her close as she would let me hug.

Am I mad? Somebody better tell me soon. Perhaps they have locked up the wrong man.

*   *

   *

No! I saw what he was trying to do!

Nussia, Nussia! No one comes. V!

And she comes trotting in. It's time. You better take her away immediately!

V says nothing, only nods her square-shaped head.

She has won, she believes. For Minnie's sake, I hope she has.

I left. I couldn't stay. Even Ford does not seem safe.

There must be a crack in what I am trying to do also. Raise up these children in a kind of paradise. Is it possible? To imagine them surrounded always—as long as we live—in our arms, Nussia's and mine. At least Mrs. V's tales of my behavior now will stop. I have done my duty: daughter, get away from me! Will the tourists treat her kindly or rough? We have seen what they can do—what you could have, had you been the man you wanted to have been. From a world that con-

123

fuses power with sin—or, better put, sin with power. And love is always sin to you, so power is just a much a part of love. Not in Hanusse! The child is loved unconditionally, whether he or she determines to return it. Ford is free. He can come and go—as he knows—as much as he pleases. Minnie. I don't know. Perhaps I have misread her. Perhaps.... We can only see. She seems so terrified of what no one has taught her to be. But she too is free. Nussia will see to that. She does not have to go with any man she does not want to. Some have many lovers every day to prevent attachment. Others one or two men over the entire summer. Occasionally a girl stays "virgin"—with regard to men. Nussia is stern, but very gentle. Why these nightmarish scenes? I must stay away for awhile. Let the children grow a bit, become what they now can without my tutelage or lack thereof. Here in Hanusse we understand when a girl changes to a woman, a boy into a man, they need a little time to digest the fact.

I miss Ford, however. In the middle of the night sometimes we awaken together and talk, very quietly, about all sorts of things: trees, plants, New York, Paris, the possibility of God without the human species—or animals at least, the incredible loneliness of a loveless life.

Leon has lived such a life. He had confused, as Americans often do, love with obedience. He had our obedience but it hadn't added up. People stood near him at all hours of day who did whatever he wanted them to: to march on a local munitions dump or suck his cock. You came and I left and you left and I came and Lizzie lay there day after day, but he felt empty nonetheless. And over the months, the years, that emptiness grew. First, he must have felt that it was *he* who couldn't experience, couldn't quite take in the thing he wanted and was being given, so he thought. So he pushed limits, upped the ante, so to speak, hoping that he might come to life amidst these more exaggerated acts. This is why depressed people sometimes push pins into their wrists, hold their fingers over flames: to try to put themselves back in touch.

Later, when that hadn't produced much more than a few heavy pants, Leon began to suspect there was something wrong with us. We weren't loving him enough. So the commands, the tests became more and more extreme. Won't you swim in the oily bay? He kept his life, but his soul was lost.

Ford interrogates me, when I grow up will I turn black?

Why do you ask that? I laugh.

Like Leon?

What do you remember of him?

I was in his arms. Held very tight. Too tight. That's all I know. I think I might have cried.

I'm sorry you remember that, I sigh.

Will I be black too?

I look into his aegean eyes. I don't know. I don't believe so.

He thinks about it for a little, resting his head upon a crooked arm: I want to be black when I get old; it will give people something to talk about.

Yes, it will that.

He has decided it and lays down to sleep again. Yes, I will be black. And Minnie will too, perhaps.

I can't help wondering, has the square-faced V been at it again? Does he have a letter hidden away some place? The B, for example, for Black. Cain could not be Abel. The blood creeps across the floor from little pools collected at the corners. The whole place smells of shit. And I sit in the center of this, keeper of my own kingdom. Bring in the suitors please. My daughter is the apple of my eye.

Is Minnie among the misses waiting now on the Quai du España? Are the Spanish sailors at this very second, giving her the eye? My apple, looking her over, with arms fraternally around each others' shoulders, licking their lips as they prepare to turn this apple into a tart. Or will she appear too awkward, clumsy, like a British schoolgirl to be in the running?

Or is she off and running away from all this herself? Take her to the Brits, V! Take her to the Brits! She will look like someone's sister, and, perhaps, a shy and sweet seaman first class, who's been buggered, by this time, by everyone on board, will find the fortitude to ask her to accompany him to the Hotel Hanusse to experience for himself what all the others have in him. Yes, V, give her to the Brits! The Spanish boys are heels with castanets.

All the time I was in Paris, I kept thinking, what if he has already sold them? Or killed them? What if they have died of malnutrition and neglect?

How had he forced you, followed you? How had he got into the place so silently and slit your throats? All the police know is that neighbors had seen the women with babies, new born, just before the murders. And that there were no other bodies at the scene of the crime. When they came to tell me, I was not shocked. He had been angry about something, almost violent about the apartment. First there was the fact that you two had disappeared, but I thought he'd gotten over that—at least enough. There was one entire weekend when he even seemed somewhat relaxed.

Fuck 'em. We'll bomb the building by ourselves!

Yes. Yes. For Leon I had no other response.

You coming to bed?

Yes. Yes.

Fuck 'em! They were just ballast.

Yes.

Come to bed!

I'm coming.

He turned, a bit desperate but amorous nonetheless.
You love me?

Yes. Yes. Only I didn't speak. We simply kissed. I kissed;
he taking over by planting his tongue in my mouth.
Nothing, as you know, was half way with him.

Screw 'em!

We did.

He put his tongue back in, less this time as a gesture of
love or the need of it than as a silent lecture.

I thought he was getting over it, getting on with whatever it was he had determined to do with life. Perhaps

129

he actually would blow up a building some day. I knew he was capable of that. What I didn't know is that he was stalking the two of you.

I didn't know why you'd gone, but I congratulated you on the act. It was the first act of self initiative that any of us had taken since we had meet Leon. It gave me hope. One day I would walk away, very far away as you apparently had. Perhaps I would return to my homeland. Perhaps…. It allowed me to dream once more.

How enormous my stupidity. Not to know that you had gone off to give birth like cats, terrified of the presence of the Tom so near the litter's nest. He not only smelled it out, knew the signs, could read the evidence, but had acquired informants (at what price I can't imagine; perhaps he also hypnotized them), had collected clues, developed a theory. His peace of mind was all pretense.

But then I began to notice in the days after how everything was upsetting him again. A fire engine could send him into a rant. Once the bells at St. Ignatius' brought out his gun as if he about the shoot down the ringer until I suggested it was probably electronically done.

One night he pushed me out of bed to the floor. You're a wimp, he barked.

I know that.

At least they've got spirit. I've got to give them that.

As I lay on the floor, a bit bruised and suddenly very sad, I was again given hope by the two of you that I too could part. I got up, and for a whole day did not return to the house. When I did return, expecting to be beaten, he was nowhere in sight. The house was so quiet—for the first time in two and a half years there were no voices to be heard, no harangues, lectures, sounds of love-making, hatching of plots, no lessons, literature read aloud, commands proclaimed, no crying from some corner, whisper or cynical remarks. Something terrible had happened—I knew that. A catastrophe had taken place as powerful as a volcano or an earthquake. It was silence, that amazing and unexpected silence, that told me everything.

Perhaps I had just needed to get away, to think for a hour or two. But I hadn't really thought. I'd gone to a couple of classes and out to attend a rally. I'd listened to every word. When I opened the door to the house, however, everything clicked. I still didn't know what happened or why, but I knew it had to do with Leon and the two of you.

When the telephone rang, I expected the worst. But it was only—how can I say *only*, given the desperation she controlled in her voice?—a friend to ask did I know where you could be reached?

No, I said, and suddenly I knew where I could. No.

Is Leon there?

No.

Oh. She paused. Please, if you know! She pleaded. She paused. I have had a very urgent call from her.

I paused. What did she say? I couldn't understand anything she said. Something about an old car. A car, evidently, she could see from a window—and a baby. My baby she said. Is she on drugs?

Could be. Did she say anybody's name?

No. Just the car and the baby. Does she have a new boy friend perhaps?

Perhaps. Goodbye.

But I'm trying to tell you, she was in hysterics!

Please. I have to make a telephone call.

Do you know where she is?

I clicked the phone dead, my hand shaking tremulously. I put my fingers into the slots of 911.

I told what I knew, what I suspected. But there was no occasion for them to check it out. Fear does not afford a police car in New York.

I called back, claiming, in another voice, I was a neighbor who had heard a gun go off. I made up a name and an address near enough. Lies obviously have more effect.

But now all I could do is wait. Wait to see if I had been correct: that the little prick Leon brought home from some froufrou bar one night had been the one to whom you'd turned in our duress, that the car you had been so troubled about was Leon's old Ford Fairlane 500. What did you mean by "baby," I pondered, rolling the sound over and over again in my mouth. Could this have expressed new found friendliness for Liz, to whom something had appeared or was just about to. You had previously always addressed her—in the cocktail waitress way you liked to imitate—as "honey," even after sex. Honey, let's get cracking before the men get in, I overheard you say one night when, unseen, I slipped back into the tunnel-like tumble of bedding and clothes we called Leon's *chambre dormé*, a room eternally asleep.

Baby. Was Leon actually in the room? Was this your final affectionate plea?

All I could do was wait. I took out my suitcase and, with candles, a broken lamp or two, and pull on the unused shade, filled the cave with light, separating my shirts, my pants—I own only about a half a dozen—from his, although we'd been wearing each other's clothing for months. In the early days, when we'd had our own apartments, I'd owned what you might call a wardrobe. Even a suit or two. Where were they now?

Probably sold off, one by one, to pay the telephone, electricity or for drugs. The house—if you remember—if memory remains in a dead body's head—was on permanent loan from one or another of Leon's nefarious actions.

I carefully folded the few articles left and gathered up what toiletries I remembered might have once been mine—an old electric razor I never used, a slightly yellowed toothbrush, a bottle of now quite coagulated shampoo. I packed these away as if they might have been treasures. They were: bits and pieces of a lost past. I became an archeologist. The pen I found under a piece of curling linoleum belonged to my father once, having been carried away with me across the seas and into this predicament. (I still write with that pen, am writing with it at this very moment!) Beneath the pillows of the couch I found a key ring. Dangling from the ring were my never returned apartment keys. Would they open that door up? Could I go there, back into the past, to find the same well-lit beige carpet and the floral settee and mahogany table that, at sunset, transformed the room from gold to roseate? A penny, it might have been mine, I left in a floorboard crack in case I had to come back—that there would still be some of me to take away.

I sat. I stood. I took the bag into the living room and leisurely, almost in slow motion, zipped it up. I sat.

If the police found something amiss, would they make the connection, check their reports and, linking name to what happened, call me back? Even visit me in a squad car? Perhaps seek out some testimony on this event. For now I was certain that an "event" of some sort had taken place. It wouldn't be long now.

I stood. I sat, turned on the television set (stolen I suspect) and looked for news. Only gameshows and soap operas. *The Days of Our Lives.* Brad is being bad to Betty who is having an affair with Brad's Dad, whose wife, killed in a car accident the year before, was *seeing* (no sex involved) Brad's uncle Teddy, who is, suspiciously, now dead.

I switched it off.

I stood, looked out the window. A neighbor boy stared at me until I dropped the curtain back. I opened it again. He touched his crotch. I turned back into the room and sat for what seemed like a month.

When the telephone finally rang, I prayed, somehow, that everything had turned out right. That perhaps it was you calling, just to say hello. Or even goodbye. You never left with a salutation. You always just went off.

It was the police. Would I come to the morgue to identify people—they couldn't say whom—I might or might not recognize. It's them I told the telephoner, who, upon giving me the address, had no further time for me and my exclamations.

I took my bag with me.

But after the identification, I came back. I had nowhere else to go. And I knew that Leon was too smart to return to his known address. I took out the little diary of phone numbers you had left behind and carefully dialed the number of your mother. It was 5:00.

She answered so hesitantly that I thought perhaps she had already heard the news. Oh, it's you, Joshua, she said. It's strange—sort of eerie actually, but I knew you were going to call me tonight—at this very hour. Something's happened to my baby, hasn't it?

I'm afraid so.

She started to cry. I'm sorry, she said.

I know. So am I.

She sobbed. Joshua, I know he did it, but I need to hear it actually said.

She was murdered.

Only silence at my own inability so say more.

Then, fortunately, she sobbed again.

Silence.

Sobs.

Will you tell the police where to send the bodies?

Bodies?

Yes, send Liz along as well?

So you knew?

138

No. It just had to happen, knowing what you and she had told me. Then, this afternoon, the house got so silent (as it always does), but it was different. I was waiting for your call.

I'm sorry. I'm sorry. So sorry. Now I was sobbing too.

I know. You didn't know, she and you, what you were getting into.

The line went dead. She hung up, I suspect, so she could cry without, metaphorically speaking, having to wipe my eyes.

When the phone went dead, however, my tears immediately disappeared, and a wave of nausea arose in my chest. The police would be here soon, I said to myself. But they were late, not arriving until nearly ten o'clock.

Given the circumstances, they were very nice. At the precinct I told the detective everything I knew—and they told me what I had not. I knew now not only who "baby" was, but of their involvement with "one named Peter Middleton." He is either dead, I said, or has gone where Leon has.

You know this gentleman?

He may be dressed as a woman.

There I stood at the door of the 115th precinct head-
quarters of the Manhattan police, my little black bag
in tow and no where to go. I didn't have more than a
ten. I almost turned back to ask, could you lock me
up? But I wouldn't have survived if they laughed.

The house was impossible. Already there were ghosts.

When I looked out the window, there was no neighbor boy, just a policeman circling the block. I was safe.
I did not sleep nonetheless.

Where? Where had he taken the children? My children too? Perhaps my children alone. For Lizzie (you
would never have confided anything to me that might
have strengthened my position or even given me
strength) had once admitted that Leon was—to put it
politely—not as virile as he once was.

Where?

I awoke confused, unable to recognize where I lay. I can't say why. I was used to the living room floor. When Leon wanted you or wanted Lizzie and Lizzie or you didn't want me, that was where I spent the night. Yet I awoke completely unacclimated, lost. I tried to stumble in the direction of the bathroom, but in the dark I hit the closet door instead. My whole sense of direction was completely "turned around" (does this make sense in any language other than American?) I was in the kitchen now. I still hadn't had anything to eat. So I cooked an egg and, upon its completion, threw it down the drain untouched. I felt so satiated I wanted to vomit it all up. I found the floor again—my little patch of it—and lay back flat with arms and legs spread out from torso the way spinning women look when the men in the circus throw their knives. For an hour or more, I lay that way.

Peter, that little fag, probably had called Leon himself. Or Leon had called him up and gotten all the news. Peter had probably set it up. I'll get some ditties, girls, or Don't you silly women think of anything; we have forgotten to get milk! Then, slipping out, he'd pressed the lever on the lock, leaving an open door only between Leon and you four. Wherever Leon had taken the babies, he would need a nursemaid. Peter must have waited in the car, a far crueler act than the actual tear of flesh through the knife. The fairy queen gone absolutely rancid on a little girl's birthday cake. And you *were* girls, weren't you? Scared, confused, but giggling still in the anticipation of what each day might present.

The cat came in to sit on the center of my stomach. I had to laugh, realizing what a sight the two of us might have been had someone suddenly turned on the lights.

Yes! I jumped up. Yes! Peter had once claimed he was a hustler in Montmartre, to which Leon had quipped, In Paris you must be able to sell anything!

I quickly put on my clothes, called Nicky from a pay phone down the street. I'll do a run for you if you just give me money for the trip. You can't come to the house. You can buy my ticket and tell me what to do at JFK. Air France. This morning. Now or never, bitch!

* *
*

It's not really blood on the old dance floor, but water leaking from some nearby well; rotting what is left of the floor boards, rusting out the joints of the aluminum walls where they meet the concrete. But in the dark…in the moonlight…..

You hated my imagination most. Perhaps I imagined the entire scenario—and you went off with Leon, Peter with Liz. Perhaps I couldn't accept the facts. I have to admit, to this day I couldn't tell you where the morgue in Queens is. We are such an unsure folk.

I'm going back to my little brood tomorrow—no I shall return today. I'm bored, lonely, need their faces for the reassurance I exist. Will Minnie be already large? Will she know what is happening?

I trust Mrs V to that: Nussia the nurse who will rub her tummy every night. Certainly they will now be sleeping in the same bed and we will have an extra corner to put up the memorial to Liz and you I have been plotting in my head. It is time the children knew—not all the gory details yet, but the facts—as I have, at least, imagined them.

No one was in the house. I sat to write a bit, but couldn't bring myself to say more than this. I slept, a nightmare in result. I was in a room, a very large one, but I was also outside of it, looking in. There I was! I recognized myself and some men, who appeared to be interviewing me. And then I was within again. Where did you put it? the tall man asked.

What?

Is it on the table? the short one continued.

What?

Is it under the bed? the tall one again interrogated me.

What?

Is it in the kitchen perhaps?

What?

Is it behind the door? Tell me if I'm getting hot.

So it continued on and on, the naming of all the places IT might have been without my being able to say anything but ask, over and over, what IT was.

Eventually they went away, and I was looking in at myself once more. Only I, too, had evidently left. So

I—the other I—the voyeur, entered the large, dark chamber. Just as suddenly, the tall and the little man were back, about to interrogate me again.

Is it in your pocket? asked the tall one, sliding his hand into it.

Is it in your shirt? asked the little one, who, as soon as he said it, had already unbuttoned my blouse and was poking about.

Is it in your pants? the tall one asked, who, having already unbuttoned and unzipped, was circling my private parts.

Is it in your ass? the dwarf darkly giggled, which, as you will have guessed, he was thoroughly inspecting at that very moment.

Is it in your mouth? As his passed his fingers through my lips, I quickly closed my teeth tight. There! There it is, he cried out! And they were all over me, prodding and poking and pulling and pummeling and punching and yes, pleasing me as much as punishing me for whatever it was I had done.

145

They suddenly stopped. You are an imposter, the big man said. You are not yourself!

You are an imposter, added the little one. You are someone else!

I am me, I pleaded.

You are not me! exploded the giant.

I am not you! shouted the midget.

I know that! But I am I.

Prove it! they demanded in one breath.

I was stunned. Dreamers seldom have passports—and I was no exception.

Look at this face, I shouted. It's mine. These eyes, this nose, these lips, chin, ears, neck. No one else on the earth has these.

The big one took out a measuring stick. In his hands, the small one had some sort of chart.

Jaw?

Contrary.

Chin?

Oval.

Lips?

The upper is Linguistic.

The lower?

Amative.

The cheek?

Artistic.

Nose?

Straight.

Medium.

Short.

Downward.

Round.

Red.

Breath.

The eyes?

Conjugal.

They compared notes, turned to me, and pronounced:
You are not who you think you are!

Who am I then?

If I told you, you would not believe me, said the towering figure.

So, said the squatting toad, you have no reason now
to doubt.

Next!

Just as quickly, I was put out—where to I can't say, for I awoke. The house was dark, in an empty hush. Had V taken the children to Megos for a visit to her sister?

I turned on the lights. For the first time I noticed the condition of the house: overturned chairs, the dishes in the sink still undone. V was not exactly clean, but she was punctilious when it came to household tasks. Never had I known her not to give the dishes, at the very least, a quick rinse. In the corner lay the sprawled torso of Minnie's doll.

I was in Hanusse City as fast as my feet could carry me there. I saw immediately what my mind had not accounted for. It was the Carnival, one of five held throughout the summer to keep the tourists busy, entertained. For its—the city's, the country's, the economy's—survival depends on the participation of almost everyone and the attendant traveler's checks in the dance about the city walls. The citizens dress in theatrical and, often, extravagantly revealing costumes and dance about while the tourists stand away a bit to observe the clumsiness of it. We have no local dances, so we merely make it up—waltz, polka, rhumba, twist and tango all in one. Eventually, we get the sailors and college boys from Britain, France, and Germany to join in, and the atmosphere gradually is transformed from theater to the festival announced. Bands play, confetti is tossed.

Had the children simply convinced the V to join them in this? Previously they had abhorred it, Ford because of its lack of grace; Minnie for its enforcement of fun. Even if the sex had introduced an element of pleasure into her previously painful life, Minnie couldn't have changed as much as that! I cannot even imagine Ford among these prancing oafs. V herself put the word to these events which characterized all of our positions: It is a *turdity*, she pronounced. She may have meant *absurdity*; I was so pleased with her designation, I never asked.

But I knew—I *know*, since I now sit at a café where I write this to you—that they were/are here, that this is the only place to escape. They had to get to people quick, mill in among them, blend.

No! I shouted. No!

*   *
*

I remember the very first time I kissed him. He was surprised, delighted, and fell passionately into the act. He had very soft lips that he manipulated marvelously to fit whatever you put through. A tongue could get lost in the cavern of his mouth. You know all of this! But I hope to understand how such a man, a truly tender man too, could do what he did. In sex he was not at all so self-assured as he was in daily life; he invited you—carefully of course—but inevitably into himself. Man and woman both he kept the shift in perfect balance between invitation and entrance. You would always find yourself surprised by him. But when it was done, it was as if he could no longer bear you for a second more. He might even leave the house. Or call up someone and invite them over as quickly as they could come. Another person's presence was required.

That was a crack as well. A fissure so deep that it kept away the very ones whom he wanted so desperately to draw to him, "draw" him so to speak, create him, make him up. You particularly refused to participate in that. When he was strong you sat at his feet, you disappeared when he was weak. It was no wonder that the more the cracks in his personality came together to become a tear, the less you were there. I should imagine it would have come to a departure even without the children.

You and Liz got pregnant to keep him—and me too—at arm's length. Even though your bellys weren't yet big, you grew large in the knowledge of it. I mistook your selfishness for brave acts. But he knew, must have known all along, what you were up to. At first, it didn't matter much, since he had long since become impotent. And you were still there to do his bidding, with regard to politics. When you refused to join our little sit-in at the Flushing Induction Center, however, he recognized the end was in sight. One more picnic. One more wild night. When those failed as well, neither you (and Liz) or he had any other choices left. I was the only one who did not know the course of future events.

What if I had left? It might have changed everything, drawn fire away from the two of you. Brought energy—even hate—back into Leon's life. For he didn't hate you, I'm certain of that. It was pain, a disintegration of the self, that permitted him to pull the knife across your necks. And now he had to clean up the evidence. Not for the police. The bloody bodies were all there. But for himself. The babies in his arms were identities he had forever lost. How they ever got them through customs and the airplane trip is beyond my imagination. Peter probably just packed them into his knapsack and poured a little milk into their mouths when the plane went dark. Did Minnie, did Ford not fuss, not cry out once? Perhaps he had a stewardess as an ally. Where did he get the money for the trip? Nicky must have thought he was going to get very rich with all of us so suddenly willing to smuggle cash in for cocaine out. Leon could, however, have had another source. Someone in the airlines, in the government even. Did he have a passport or—as in my dream— was his face alone enough.

The crowd continues winding down the narrow streets. I want to wander, follow, run to the sides and front of the kind of conga line it has become. But it would only draw Leon all the quicker to them. I sip a little more of my Campari.

That is what I drank in all the cafés of Paris. Imagine me trying to play the detective in a city of that size. I was as scientific as one can be about finding a flea in a field of Kansas corn (I have stolen all your metaphors).

I inhabited at first the most American of spots: St.-Germain-des-Prés, the Deux Magot, the Latin Quarter, Jardin des Tuileries. Everywhere the photograph received the famed Parisian shrug. My query concerning the sale of little girls and boys took me from the Camelon to the Cave Outre. Le temps perdu—and fast! Soon I knew Nicky's friends would be after me, and they'd have no difficulty following my tracks…. I had left the footprints of a Bigfoot. If I could encounter them—and survive it—perhaps they would lead me to Leon.

The days were always cool and sunny in my little L'Hôtel (Oscar Wilde's old bedding spot) with a beautiful view across of carpenters who, observing my attentions, flexed their muscles and bent their butts, but wouldn't touch what I was trying telepathically to tell them to.

Each day I visited a quarter different from the day before. I began always at the edges, circling it, and then, rue by rue, allée by allée, closed in on the heart, where generally a church stood surrounded by three or four cafés. In one of these I sat for the rest of the day.

It was like a game, a game we have here in Hanusse. Someone draws a circle and stands at the very center of it. Someone outside leans in with their chalk to draw a little circle near the edge.

Your mother's name is….they have to guess….Anne.

Yes.

Then they can enter it. Another does the same.

Your father's name is….this goes on, circle after circle, square after square, triangle after triangle, through rectangles and even parallelograms until around the oracle's very feet a heart is drawn. And you love…. Some dare to say their own names.

I was surprised that no one had come up and put a gun to my head. They must have been following. Perhaps, they thought, I would eventually lead *them* to Leon—that is if he too had taken money from Nick.

It was all too peaceful and pleasant. I ordered wine and the glass broke in my mouth, spilling the red substance all over my hands and tablecloth. Something was going to happen which only I could prevent.

One day I was walking down rue Sebastopol, a seedy, slightly sinister part of the city. On rue Rambuteau, I turned right and right again immediately at rue

Quincampoix, a very narrow street upon which sits a little porno shop. I was about to go in, but just before entering, looked up. Overhead sat a man in a window, enjoying a cigarette. It was the drug lord of Queens, Nicolar Theogrippas. For a moment I thought he saw me as I darted in the porno place. Inside, the manager tried to interest me in something he held beneath the counter, seeing my obvious disinterest, evidently, in his featured products. I demurred and went out again quick, crossing the street with bent head. When I could look up, Nick had disappeared. I found a little bar nearby that had a window view.

If you do not know Paris, this will seem a strange co-incidence, a novelistic leap in a desperate author's search for plot. If you know Paris, you will understand that you are destined to run into someone you know— if you walk the streets long enough. In tracking down Leon, I had depended on this fact. The figure I had come upon, however, confused me utterly. Had Nick come after Leon himself? As he sat, smoking a Gauloise, eyes slightly closed in complete repose, he suggested a man who had obtained what he wanted, a stance which, back in the good ole USA, I'd never seen him take. Was Leon within as well? And, if so, what was their relationship?

Perhaps he had simply put two and one together: Leon was flying to Paris and I was trying to get there and the girls had been found with slit throats. Or was I the object of my own chase? A link in Leon's past that the knife needed still to snip. The children, me—and he was free! Free, after the inevitable passing of Peter and, now perhaps, Nick. Only your mother, so far away and so unlikely to intrude, knew the facts. Did she really know I was going to call at precisely 5:00?

There were too many contradictions. I could have been done away with a week before, the children smothered en route. What was happening?

* *
*

Let us start all over again. Dear Hannah, I am here. I'm always here. The children are fine.

* *
*

They're in danger. When I had Leon committed, I never imagined they would let him out! Cured?! No one in Hanusse has ever used such a word before. We do not believe in health! Evil is evil eternally. Good is good because it is not bad. As Ricochet wrote: A good act is one which an evil one would commit if he could, but, not having the ability, hates the human race, enacting upon others what can be understood as punishment for their inability to accept the gesture in which he has failed. Murder, accordingly, is a criminal's good deed, since, in the evil mind, good, the way it is defined, lies beyond his capacities.

What are my capacities for evil, for good? My dream, obviously, projects a sense of guilt. I am not as blameless as I suppose myself, says my Id. My Ego, however, objects to all this. The first self of my sleep fable admitted—he must have—to some small role in the series of events, and so is freed, but the self lying in passivity denies its implication in any way and has, thus, created two diametrically opposed aspects of itself to force the Ego into facing the reality:You are not who you think you are! Despite all of this, however, it (the Ego) knows it did not commit the act and, perhaps, could have not have committed it; and is, accordingly, given, in the midst of its condemnation, a blessing of sorts: You will have no doubts.

The dream, however, lies to the dreamer even as it speaks the truth. For after a judgment of this sort doubts arise in full force. It's as if God were to tell you, you have been completely honest, when you knew you had not. Only the liar would understand this as praise; the honest would recognize it as a severe chastisement—unless one perceived God as an utter idiot, in which case, one would have to oneself be an idiot to have accepted such a deity.

I search the crowd for the recognizable trio without success. Please, spare them God. Perhaps Leon is now sane and has left the soil of Hanusse to the crazy ones who hang on like the naked nut trees stuck along our mountain paths.

I didn't really know if Leon was in France, and now I'm equally unsure whether V, Ford, and Minnie have escaped into the pageant against which I have played all my chips, a bet, "women's intuition" you told me it was.

Women's intuition. Do men not have such a thing? They recently reported in *Scientific American* that women use both chambers of their brain, men only one, so that women think simultaneously in logical terms and intuitive ones. Men rely too much on logic or facts.

Not I! Still, I have to admit, I make a ridiculous dick. I sat at that café, just as I sit at this one, for hours and hours. The cafés close at 12:00 in the 2nd arrondissement. I fell to sleep, I was drunk.

*   *
*

At home (my little hotel home) I took a long, hot bath, trying to puzzle out the significance of what I thought I'd witnessed. No new insights. I slept as peacefully as I had on every night in France. The workers whistled me awake, and witnessed me without a stitch through the open door of le balcon. One took his shirt off, the others bent down with butts up in the air to, presumably, sand the floor. It was a little ritual with us: a game, a way for confirmed heterosexuals to play out homosexual sex without actualizing it.

I dressed and went out. On my way to rue Quincampoix I bought a pocket knife. The bar at the corner of rue de la Reynie had the perfect vantage point. But I saw nothing all that day. No one came, no one went away. Night was no different. 22 rue Quincampoix seemed to house people who never arrived or never left.

I took a hot bath.

Is that Minnie up ahead? In the pilgrim hat?

On the third day, my nerves were all a mess. I sweated profusely in the humid air, and when it began to rain I had to go inside to sit by the window where the view was ever so slightly obscured. In those hours I decided to take notes for a future when I might write down—as I have been doing for you—everything that transpired.

A dog came up to me and I pet it for awhile. Here in Hanusse, a cat has come to sit in my lap. Animals always seem to find comfort in my presence. Even the filthy pigeons of Paris came right up to my chair. That must stand for something. The innocent, at least, are not scared off.

No one arrived and no one left.

I had to return to my little table on the rue de la Reynie; I had no where else to go.

I ordered Campari and took one sip before the door across opened to quickly close; not totally, however. I got up, crossed the street and pushed it open. In the foyer there was no one. I climbed the stairs. On the third floor I stopped. Leon used to have a way of knocking, a sort of private code, more habitual than significant: three short taps and a little dance of the fingers, half way between a nervous tic and scratch. I imitated his knock. The door opened straight away revealing a figure that took me a few seconds to recognize as Liz. You were on the couch. I turned around as if to leave (do you remember that?), I was so abashed. Then I turned back and entered into the room, the knife already in my hands.

* *
*

Here come another sequence of celebrants, doing some sort of Bulgarian peasant kick, a foot each side and a slap on the buttocks of the person whom you're following. The Americans get giddy with this act, thrilled and embarrassed to be doing something naughty as it feels nice.Kick kick, slap. Kick kick, slap.

I must have passed out was the first thing I thought upon coming to. I didn't imagine that I'd just gone through my own version of "kick kick, slap."

Nicky must have been there all along, waiting, knowing I would come, had to go through that door. Pure curiosity. Perhaps even leaving clues…subtle ones… no, obvious tracks! When I think back…when, spread out in the middle of that drawing room, I tried to understand how I had been so easily led to the mysterious Quincampoix, drawn to it even…I hurt, could not think any longer, fell back into black. But then, upon coming to again, I seemed to recall, in a single flash, your back, the shape of your neck. And then I knew, in another instant, everything! Why you and Lizzie had left, why Leon had seemed at the time of your leaving so relatively resigned to the fact. All had been plotted, planned, charted, checked and double-checked. You were not victims but participants in some grander plot, where the victim was so ignorant, so naive, so selfish, stupid, sentimental, silly, just plain dumb, that he could not even imagine his predicament, not comprehend that he was the object of a magnificently ridiculous test—a trial of almost mythic proportions. My dream had tried to tell me everything.

It had not been *your* devotion and love Leon doubted—drugs and desperation had ensured that—but my *own*. I was the drifter, the one who no longer fit into the pattern he had projected for (upon) us.

I now recall when we first moved in with him, a still loving couple (*still* in love in both senses), afraid of joining his little clan (the Sharon Tate murder was soon to take place), and yet eager to participate in such a *noble experiment*. I had more doubts than you, was not completely ready to relinquish all semblance of thought. But you spoke, as you did always, with a greater sense of sarcasm. I was all belief, so was a bit more cautious in the deity's transference. You, who believed in little, as you insisted, appeared to be more independent, but were, in actuality, more hooked, more caught up in his myth.

Leon liked them that way: doubters in whom he could inspire faith. Those with natural faith were more difficult to cultivate. That was the biggest crack of all—a whole chasm in fact. All the time I perceived myself as a bridge! Stupid, sentimental, selfish, dumb. In a typhoon the bridge generally washes away. The frighted and fatigued fellow travelers huddle in a clean, well-lighted room (you see, I remember some of my English studies!).

Ricochet describes the process: "When myth meets human necessity it generally gives way, and it is at that very moment when myth begins to self-destruct. There are many explanations for its transformation; but whether it be described as a process of continuing revelation, reformation, or generative insight, it is always the beginning of the end of faith. For myth, as he has said, in order to *be* myth, must be grounded in an unquestioning t(h)rust. All genuflexions to the exigencies of daily human life are not merely heretical, but secure myth's death. Even though the faithful may continue to assert its validity, the very fact that the myth has undergone transformation testitfies to its inability to sustain."

I was all belief. There was little left for the rest of you but doubt. And as I came to, with faces gradually revealing themselves over my prostrate protestations, it was as if suddenly I were witnessing the spectres of my past as it is rumored to before the eyes of a dying man. But these were real faces—not projections of one's imaginative past—and death was possibly a few

165

mintues off. As a beloved convert I might be given one last chance. I was. Leon's large and now strangely lethargic frame leaned over me for closer inspection. What did he see in my eyes?

I heard the babies cry and quickly be comforted. I saw a second of deep compassion—even love perhaps—before hate came crashing down upon my brain.

Kick kick, slap. Left for dead, there was no one to witness my resurrection.

*   *
*

Of a sudden I spot…I turn away. I cannot…must turn back…and back again to the tabletop. It is our little girl, my love, with six Russian sailors! And she…I cannot believe it, is all in giggles over them. I want to stand, go over to these burly beasts and demand my daughter back, as if there were a back to which one could return.

For suddenly I realize how savvy Mrs. V has been to bring Minnie out in the company of all the revelers about. With the Russians she will be safe. Even Leon would not dare attempt to wrest a young woman from a bear cave. The Italians might have been distracted, the French talked out of it, the Spanish lulled by song, the Brits convinced it was their duty to give her up. The Americans would already be searching for someone to whom they could pass her (and their guilt) on. But these Russians will huddle and hide their treasure until they sail off. Will a Tartar boy satisfy the father Ford must become?

Where, I wonder *is* Ford? And will Leon recognize the baby nearly become a man? I shudder at the thought.

Was it woman's inutition or had I overheard some words? For I knew then—on that Paris floor—where I could find the infants, as if I had secretly (even to myself) known all along where everything would end, without being able to locate the place in space. It was almost dark, just a slip of sun that darkens Paris against its own lights for a few seconds on November nights.

These are the cemeteries of Paris: Père Lachaise, Montmartre, Passy, Montparnasse, Batignolles, and, of course, the Pantheon, Saint-Étienne and other Paris churches. Which one?

*The Zolas had left Medan to return to Paris, in large part
because of Emile's ongoing toothache. On the morning of
September 28th they arrived at their Paris home. The valet
was asked to light the fire, since both Emile and Alexandrine were chilled to the bone. Both were equally quite
tired, in part because of the continued hostilities surrounding the Dreyfus affair—garbage, for example, was
often hurled at their carriage—and because of Emile's
recent taxing work of* Vérité (Truth), *just completed.*

*At about 3:00 AM Emile awoke, feeling nauseous. Alex-
andrine did not feel well either. But Emile, often prone to
indigestion, did not wish to bother the servants. Later
Alexandrine awoke quite ill, and, near unconsciousness,
could not help her husband, who had fallen to the floor.
She, herself, quite overcome, fell back into the bed. Because of her husband's fears of violent intrusion, the doors
had been bolted from within.*

*Although assassination was suspected (and even ru-
mored), the cause of death according to the coroner's report was carbon monoxide poisoning, asphyxiation. De-
cades later a right-winged anti-Dreyfusian reported that*

he and other workers had taken tile from a neighboring chimney and placed it as a block to the chimney of the Zola's house. The truth has never been determined.

Zola was buried in 1902 in the cemetery at Montmartre.  *But in 1908 his body was dug up and moved to the Pantheon, despite right wing protests. At the ceremony a man attempted to assassinate the attending Alfred Dreyfus, who caught hold of the man's arm and forced him to surrender the gun.*

[SOURCE: *Zola: A Life*, by Frederick Brown (New York: Farrar, Strauss, Giroux, 1995).

*   *
*

For months Piaf had been very ill from years of bodily neglect, wine and drugs. The chiropracter, Lucien Vaimber, had improved her condition, but she was in a fragile state still—and lonely. Claude Figus, for a time Edith's secretary and jester (he was imprisoned for frying eggs, just to amuse her, over the eternal flame of the Arc de Triomphe), had "discovered" the young Greek hairdresser, Théophanis Lambouskas, in January 1962, and took the boy to dinner at Piaf's boulevard Lannes home. He was invited back, and soon after visited Piaf with Figus at the Neuilly clinic where she was suffering from bronchial pneumonia. She was in strong spirits and was obviously falling in love with the handsome young Greek, of whom she demanded that he change his family name to Sarapo, "I love you." It was almost as if Claude, a one time lover with obvious bisexual leanings, were arranging for an affair between Théo and Edith. And suddenly, as she prepared for a new concert tour, Théo was very much the focus of her plans: he must lose a little weight, be in perfect physical condition (Vaimber assured her of that), and must, most importantly, be taught to sing and act.

In Cannes, the suite at the Hôtel Majestic was shuttered: she disapproved of sunlight. And there journalists sought her out to feed them sensational news in the midst of the summer slump. She readily signed an announcement of her marriage to Sarapo, which Théo had written out in his own hand.

In Nice, Monaco, and Cannes, Edith and Théo performed. The young man was appreciated by the audiences, particularly when he sang his songs without a shirt.

In late September they perfomed at Olympia in Paris for two weeks, a period which she survived only through an ingestion of pills and injections of Coramine. On October 9th they married at the Greek Orthodox Church in rue Darnu. The groom was twenty-seven years younger than the bride.

After a performance in Brussels, Piaf was again hospitalized for pneumonia and liver damage. Théo rented a villa near Cap Ferrat for her recovery, but after a visit to another clinic, they moved to a smaller villa near Grasse.

Every weekend, Théo came down from Paris, on one visit bringing her the news of Claude's death by an overdose of drugs. Piaf lived increasingly in a state of confusion and fantasy, at times finding it impossible to speak, at other times madly planning her comeback.

On the early morning of October 10th, 1963 Piaf's nurse noticed that her patient was hemorrhaging internally. She administered the serum, called the doctor and a priest. At 5:10 Piaf died. Her dear friend, Jean Cocteau,

171

who had written Le Ball Indifférant *as a vehicle for her acting talents, died the same day, possibly in response to the news of her death.*

Piaf was buried in Père Lachaise in the 97th division near Paul Éluard and Amedeo Modigliani. Seven years later, Théo Sarapo died in an automobile crash near Limoges, and was buried with his wife.

[SOURCE: *Piaf*, by Margaret Crosland (New York: Fromm International Publishing Corporation, 1987). Published originally in 1985 by Putnam Publishing Group.]

*   *
*

One day I went walking with Ford. We often play a game, just the two of us, that purposely mystifies logic.

I cannot remember how the game got started. Perhaps I was attempting to explain aspects of Western thought and something went terribly astray. In any event, we were playing this game that day.

> Ten indians do not a tribe make.
> Twenty indians not a nation.
> Two apples do not bake a cake.
> A pound of rye does not a pie.
> Three crows no parliament.
> Four cardinals not a college.
> Fifteen collegians do not make a pope.
> But the sixteenth might!
> Ten mothers cannot make a baby.
> Two boys do not make a man.
> Two fathers do not make a son.

I looked over to see if there was something behind his statement. There was.

And two women do not raise a daughter right! He nearly shouted in a strange mix of fear and liberation. And with that he ran ahead fast.

Come back! I whispered to myself. Come back! Clearly

V had been talking again, filling his little head with her suspicions and half-truths—and had gotten terribly near the mark.

Do you want a mother? I called out.

Not now! he answered over his shoulder.

> The past does not the future make.
> The future cannot redeem a past.

These lines, Ricochet's, not my son's, suddenly came to me, watching him dart off.

*   *
*

Ten or twelve nearly naked boys and girls come dancing past. Loincloths, a few beads dangled across the breasts—they symbolize American Indians, and trouble American tourists, some of whom (wives in particular) turn away with faces flushed red. Others laugh at the audacity of the children while simultaneously oogling the lines and contours these dancing bodies project. The Italians applaud. Some Brazilians jump up to participate. The Greeks rub their bellies,

174

the Spaniards each other. Only the Russians remain disinterested, although one has an erection and appears to be drooling a bit.

Next several geisha, a couple dozen—all young men in drag. A camel or two, with humps of human buttock. Applause, laughter, gasps.

We are the sirens.

I blink and when I look back the Russians are no longer where they sat. Minnie, too, has disappeared into the little hotel room they have rented in which to perform their sexual acts. God bless you, dear. I remembered her doll on the floor of our house, dropped apparently in the hasty rush to escape the place.

We are not always here and not always well. In the bushes I vomit up everything I have drunk. I have a fever perhaps.

The Flat, High Nose. The Dimpled Cheek. The Dyspeptic One. The Agreeable Eye. The Inquisitive Eye. The Conjugal. The Amative Lip. The Conscientious Cheek. All dance about me in my delirium.

We are everyone!

*   *
*

Beckett was aging. He had serious respiratory problems. His legs hurt. And when he fell at his apartment in boulevard Saint-Jacques, his wife said she could no longer care for him. His doctor placed him in a nursing home at Tiers Temp.

There he had a simple room painted blue with a bed of iron, a wardrobe, and writing desk. A single tree graced a small courtyard, where he fed pigeons until workers appeared with their canvas and scaffolds to renovate the place.

At first he returned occasionally to blvd. St.-Jacques, but gradually he retreated more and more to his room at the home, cordially greeting the other tenants on his frequent walks to Parc-de-Montsouris down boulevard Raspail across Place Denfert-Rochereau—an intersection which terrifies the most blasé of pedestrians—to the avenue René Coty, which runs directly into the park. His legs were hurting badly more and more often. He had finished writing with the composition Stirrings Still when Suzanne died, July 17th, 1989. He was now waiting for his own death.

176

One December noon he entered the dining room and begin walking up and down beside the tables, gesturing and speaking fast. An ambulance was called. From the stretcher he shouted, "I will be back!"

At the hospital he fell into a coma, and, on the 22nd of December, died. The day after Christmas his body was interred,  *without a priest, at the Cimetière du Montparnasse.*

[SOURCE: *Samuel Beckett: The Last Modernist,* by Anthony Cronin (London: Flamingo/Harper-Collins, 1997).]

*

Then. At that time I thought I was choosing randomly. For you see, I had suddenly no belief at last. You—Leon, Liz, Hannah—had depended upon that, for otherwise you—Leon, Nick, and Peter the poof—would have slit my throat. No, you had always depended upon the belief that belief can be wiped out, washed away. It is always the nonbeliever's first tenant of faith: believing is a dirty business and must, from time to time, be hosed down. The true believer must be forced to come to his senses. For unlike myth, politics is—I quote Ricochet again—"entirely about the exigencies of everyday experience, and as such, transformation is at its very heart. The best politician is a sort of transformer, in the sense of one who changes things and something (hardly a human being in this rôle) that receives an electrical charge, converts its energies, and sends it back out. 'He is the voice of the people.' To believe anything too thoroughly or for too long a period is most dangerous. Whenever zealots get involved with politics, they terrorize the art. Unable to perceive that the most effective political being is he who does not believe the same thing twice—or (as the Portuguese say) 'a strong king does not stand on the same balcony for more than two days'—the zealot must maim, torture, and murder to get his way. While the true politican puts the path before the donkey and the cart. As the Romans—brilliant politicians as recognized today—knew, if you want to march a legion, pave the way."

You thought you'd stamped out my religious instincts with your little travesty of murder. But there I was again in Paris, like a wizened, wimpled nun/nothing, working my way to you once again. So you had no choice but to reveal utterly your villainy. And that finally succeeded where nothing else would.

But the gods, so it appeared, found me, even if I was stuffed up with the impossibility of everything. Not your *god*, my gods, the heathen ones, the ones in which the Hanussee trust. They came to me in my time of need and helped me to choose cemetery Montparnasse over more famous Père Lachaise.

Now, years later, I understand why it *had* to be Montparnasse where you planned to accomplish those several swaps. Montmartre would be far too hilly with babes in arms, and the entrance on avenue Rachel has attendants on both sides of it. At Père Lachaise you would be too obvious given the quantity of visitors and workman about the place. Passy and Des Batignolles are far too small. If you entered at the Rue Froidevaux gate just past the glorious apartments with windows two stories high and the walls of the building itself paneled in a spiraling pattern of flowers (it's hard to imagine how or why I remember that), you

179

might sneak past the single guard, a bit tired at 4:00; particularly if you slip in the wc to the very left of her (a Gambian woman works there many days) little station, you might wait a few minutes for a commonplace distraction. Or, if you were not afraid of drawing the attention of all school children using that route, you could enter at the farther Froidevaux porte, taking you down the avenue de l'Ouest, where there is no guard at all. Whereas, even if you entered from the rue de avenue Gambetta entrance at Père Lachaise, you'd have to cross several meters to reach the quite visible wc, which faces directly into the road. The walk to the best tombs, moreover, is a long one. No hiding infant cries in that route. Of course, you might have entered from the boulevard Ménilmontant side, not from the rue du Repos entrance but from one just to the south. But Héloïse and Abélard are near, and their great notoriety—not to mention the inappropriateness of your mission to the monument of eternal love—would make that an unlikely spot. Moreover, the best tombs for privacy are a long, uphill walk.

Now regarding Montparnasse, you might have entered from the same rue Froidevaux gate, and instead of turning left, turned to the Jewish part. It is there Alfred Dreyfus lies, having spoken the truth throughout his life. But the stones there are, for the most part, low, with only an avenue or two of larger tombs. Although, if you were to have chosen a spot up against the wall of avenue Thiery in Division 30, you might have gotten away with it. Up a little and over from Vercours.

But Nicky knows his cemeteries, I have to grant him that. God knows he's put enough people into them. But a confederate probably arranged your Paris itinerary. Nicky knows Queens, in both senses of that word, not urbane citizens of the city of light. Someone certainly knew exactly what to do.

In rue Quincampoix I stood, or at least attempted to. I seemed to be bleeding from every orifice: nose, eyes, ears, even my ass. I lay for a while, but was afraid to sleep for fear of falling into a coma. I tried to stand once more. I was fearful that if I did not soon succeed in the act, I might be there still upon your return, and Leon would kill me all over again. I crawled over to the table and, with a chair, balanced myself briefly into an upright aspect, but could not maintain the position of man's ultimate separation from the apes.

All right, I will stay here then. Let them finish me off!
I was even beginning to think in the language of film
noir! I fall for you, baby! Seems every time I run into
you kid, I fall for you in a big way. I could see you in
your stiletto heels, ever so gently poking at my adam's
apple, where a little pool of purple liquid has collected
from the rivulet that begins at my mouth.

You still living? you nonchalantly inquire.
Yep, I gulp.
Good. I was afraid he'd popped you.
Miss me?
Nope, I just wanted to know that you weren't dead
yet....so I could complete what was begun.
A gun comes out of your purple mesh purse.
See you in heaven, honey! Bang!
Again I fall.
Every time I run into you kid, I fall in a big way, I
slowly croak.

[black out]

ACT II

I have been reading what I wrote. It has taken nine-
teen years to get to this point. Act II. I was just writing

182

letters and suddenly I am wearing a back brace from all the weight of a four act play.

I am writing….that is all. To someone who could have smashed me with her shoe, with those stiletto heels you were always in (alas, not the cowhide kind, but those with vaguely human skin).

But the letters never arrived. In 1973 I read, quite by accident, of your death, your *actual* death—although by that time you had changed your name. Don't worry, I never told your mother. You were buried in Madrid, Iowa in 1969. Your mother does not read *La Stampa*, I presume?

I told you not to go to Rome! What did they do to you? And why? And who?

* *
*

In late April 1864 Charles Baudelaire arrived in Brussells, having left Paris in part because of debts (he had even to sell all rights to his translations of Edgar Allan Poe, his only regular source of income) and because he intended to write My Heart Laid Bare, *a book of rancour against*

France. Except for a brief return to Honfleurs (to beg money from his mother to help clear up his debts) and a five day stay in Paris in 1865, Charles was to remain in the city which he complained had a compulsion to wash down everything, streets and houses equally, inside and out. There he also met with his publisher, Auguste Poulet-Malassis (who himself had been exiled as a debtor), and the two planned a series of exciting new projects, including a translation of Petronius's Saytricon *and a critical work on Choderlos de Laclos.*

But Baudelaire was bored, for a time entertaining himself perhaps by attempting to reignite the flames of adulterous love between his close friend Charles Augustin Sainte-Beauve and Mme. Victor Hugo. But in the same year Baudelaire began to feel a dull pain above his right eyebrow,which gradually worsened over the weeks, developing into severe headaches and spells of dizziness. A doctor prescribed a tablet mix of opium, belladonna, digitalis and valerian. The fits grew worse, resulting in cold sweats, vomiting, distraction and stupor.

In March, on a visit to see the Eglise Saint-Loup in Rops, Baudelaire grew dizzy, fell, and suffered, the next morning, mild aphasia, asking for his already open carriage to be "open," when he quite obviously meant for it to be closed.

184

Doctors pronounced it as hysteria or a nervous disorder. Others saw more serious consequences. But only Baudelaire and his dear friend Charles Asseiseau must have known that it was syphilis in its final stages. Charles still hoped for a cure, but in late March his condition further deteriorated. His publisher wrote to Charles' mother, through her counsel, Narcisse Ancelle, that her son was in a purely vegetative state. On April 1st, Charles suffered paralysis on his right side and could no longer read or speak.

He was moved to a clinic run by Augustinian nuns, of whom even Charles' bourgeoise and unperceptive mother observed that they were "boorish," demanding that the patient cross himself and pray before being fed. Charles' irritation with their constant pestering was apparent.

On April 9th, Baudelaire turned 45. He would suffer the tortures of aphasia with paralysis—common to the syphilitic sufferer—for nearly sixteen more months, alternately enduring his mother's child-like treatment of him and his frustration for not being able fully to communicate. He was taught to say two small phrases: "The moon is beautiful" and "Pass the mustard." And occasionally, with walking cane attached to coat and the help of a companion, he took strolls, having been returned to Paris. On one such excursion, he encountered the popular novelist Ernest Feydeau. Taking Feydeau's beard with both hands, Baudelaire pulled on it tightly for a full ten minutes, murmuring the question: "hmm? humm?"

He was buried with a tomb marked also with the names of his stepfather, General Jacques Aupick (who so hated him) and the mother he spent his entire life trying to escape.

In 1949 the appeals court declared Le Fleurs du Mal *contained no obscene or vulgar word.*

[SOURCE: *Baudelaire*, by Claude Pichois, trans. by Graham Robb (London: Vintage, 1991). Originally published in England by Hamish Hamilton, 1989].

*   *

*

Let me begin all over again.

Once upon time there were events. It began, as history has always, with the slobbering snake sliding a tale into Eve's ear. The very first story recorded. And spoken by a serpent yet! Before that only commands—you shall, you shall not—shouted apparently by a jealous and understandably nervous godhead. At the very least, gentle warnings: you shall, you shan't.

But the snake had a story to tell: hisssss story, her's, ours.

Sssssay, thisssss isssssn't sssssso eassssssy for a sssssnake, sssssso lisssssten clossssse. Itsssss thosssssse persssssimonsssssss or thosssssse sssssstrawberriessssss [the fruit is unnamed] he sssssaysssss you sssssshouldn't sssssswallow sssssso sssssweet and sssssswell, well?

I was told not to eat that tasty treat. [Rhyme was easy in those days.]

Sssssso? Whosssssse tttttthere tttttto tttttell tttthee? Sssssso tttttttasssssstttty tttto sssssswallow. [Sounds like Dracula gone gay.] Tttttttasssssstttttte ittttttt! [With that little tongue darting out and in.]

And Eve just couldn't resist this vampire's swish—he bit and she too, poisoning, perhaps, the blood and spirit in the same split second.

The second story now begins.

Adam, I've been thinking.

This without a name said no.

I know, but….

Know? What does that mean? And what am "I?" Don't speak!

Well! I certainly see there are enormous differences between you and me. First of all, you don't even know who you are. That's a serious difficulty. And secondly—and most importantly I suppose—you don't know anything whatsoever! I know a thing or two, I think.

Think?

Yes, brute, think! The reason the brain was put into you!

You?

No *me*, dear. But forget it—forget everything. I want to talk about that little fruit.

Fruit?

The one with the spritely gay and slightly bitter taste [Eve's was the first advertisement for a product all could have just as well done without.]

Fruit?

Recommended by the snake.

But this without a name [pointing at himself, since he would not yet have learned to separate the world from his own being] has told us not to eat persimmons [or strawberries or whatever it was God had commanded them not to—perhaps he had meant all fruit of earth, had demanded of them simply not to eat. In Eden eating may not have been necessary.]

Oh, come on, give it a try!

[Now you must remember that Adam would have had little sales resistance.]

Why not? [He took whatever it was into his hands and bent his head in its direction.] But this without a name [pointing again at his chest] says not.

Don't be silly!

[And seeing her stamp her dainty or, if Darwin is to be believed, rather large, flat foot, he must have found her more than a little attractive.]

Okay. [And bending into the hand-held object again he—since all stories after have obsessed over the number 3, we better give humankind another chance.] Nope.

[She might have kissed him, had she known how. She probably just rubbed noses or put her paw where it felt good.] Come on!

[And Adam bit.]

[The sky darkened immediately—he probably didn't even get a taste of it.]

190

Dare you to disobey? [Gods cannot speak in normal syntax.]

[The voices in the days up until this crucial moment must have seemed to come from within as much as from without, but *this* voice was definitely from out there, in outerspace, the fact of which must have been more terrifying than the banishment it was about to impose.]

Who?

Adam, shut. Just shut up!

You—creep! [And Adam must have, in the verbal sense, gotten down and crept at least as far as the nearest tree.]

Out woman! Out man! Out of the garden!

[Woman? Man? Were they named by it with no name as something separate? Man? Woman? Their first inkling that what she had he hadn't and what he, she did not?]Oh my God! [Eve cried out.]

Oh boy! [Adam's eyes grew wide.]

Don't call me that, man! You get your ass out of here! And you, Eve, leave! [God called down, over, out.]

[The sun was about to set as they were sent—out of the garden we are told, but not what that "outside it" existed of—desert, meadow, plain, an ocean perhaps (much more of the world was water in those days). It was the first murder mystery, one might say. For in every philosophical, psychological and religious sense, the expulsion signifies their death. Since we're still here we must suppose that, for a while at least, they survived in their new Siberia, begetting a bundle of brats (the perception of their *différence* mean *sex* in those days, and little else.) It seems a shame the story was not more specific. What was their world like? Much like ours today, I suspect. But then, what was the garden? I think of Rousseau—but it must have been far better than what we know of art if the deity put so much faith in it and so punished those who could not. Certainly it was no simple jungle. It was the closest thing to heaven that living beings have ever experienced, although, as we have shown, they were rather dumb to it all. It is in the genetic codes of Eve's memory only that we can have any rational memory. For only she ate the fruit of knowledge and had, however brief it may have been, a little time to ponder it, to take in what she (they) were about to give up.

Of course, my feeling has always been, given my status as a born believer, if the world the way we know it was Eve's doing—as impossible and horrible, terrifying and cataclysmic as it all has been—one has to give credit to the old girl. It's been fun! Although, if I had been a victim of the holocaust, if I had suffered the inquisition, if I had had to witness the slaughter of the innocents, or even lived in Alexander's path, in Caligula's Rome, been a slave to Tutakamen, had I had Beckett's doubt, I might have offered Adam one or two more denials. Or given Eve a better part—Salome at least. (Salome was, in fact, a precursor of its author's evolution: pure love to mad murderess, caustic wit to pedarast, was the very thing for which one is worshipped at same time for which one is whipped.)

But Eve, poor Eve, damned to eternity by doing what came quite naturally: thinking, eating, sharing—all at the root of her eventual act of child-bearing. I think therefore I eat—and you are hungry too? Save some of the baby, please!

For *that* the deity damned us all to perdition? Saved us? Led us into temptation—or, at least, allowed us to be led? I'm not sure I like this Godhead.

Perhaps there is another one to whom I should subscribe. Ricochet deals with that dilemma: "Given all I have written about the absoluteness of faith required for a myth to survive, the reader will be surprised to hear me admit that faith is not at all what religion is about. The myth may be claimed as any church's theology, but that seldom has to do directly with the myth. My tenets may require you to bow, but if you come to our church week after week, you may sit. Perhaps you have rheumatism or a crick in the neck. A chaplain could bury Edith Piaf, not a priest. Religion seldom preaches what and to whom it can teach. Think of the Jesuits! Religion like politics permits transformation, but simply at a far slower pace, so it may pretend (even to itself) that there has been no alteration at all. The priest, monk or layman, accordingly, does not recognize the hypocrisy of the institution. From without it is obvious, but seldom from within.

So it is with all religions: the believer within may severely doubt, but for the doubter without, his inability to believe is a sin. A convert, accordingly, is required (most often by himself) to believe more firmly than the born believer, while the believer, baptized as a baby, is permitted (by both the institution and himself) to mock his faith, abuse and ignore it—as long as he returns, from time to time, to the flock. Church leaders will deny this; from a theological standpoint (from their positions as the keepers of the myth) they necessarily must. But in actuality, the saved are always saved, the damned, damned. Calvin knew this was true.

God loves, evidently, as a tribal mother might. Her children may be angering, but they are, nonetheless, hers and consequently are forgiven again and again. An adoptee may occasionally apply, but for the rest of the world there is no embrace. Hence the harangues of fundamentalists: Stay away or I'll shoot if you're not a member of my house.

Meanwhile, inside (inside the community and the self) you can behave as you want—as long as it's not too obvious and you don't get caught. The very act of behaving as a "heathen" (the name for outsiders) is absolutely delicious to God's special kids.

It is no accident that the most profound questioners of faith have been unquestionably born into the clan:

Socrates, Buddha, Jesus, Mohammed, Augustine, Leonardo, Darwin, Freud, Beckett, and Lenny Bruce. If only Eve and Adam could have had a family in Eden religion might have protected them from God's wrath."

Then what is evil? I've seen it; I know it when I see it, but it remains something indefinite. Perhaps it is the very nature of evil not to be comprehended. Is it beyond, above, about—outside of ourselves, our tribe, our house? But we know that cannot be so. We know because the only thing we truly know of it is the fact that occasionally or often or seldom sometimes it is something seen in ourselves. I am certain that is how we recognize it—if it is possible to recognize it—in the surrounding space we describe as our planet.]

*   *
*

You might have chosen Passy, Nicky or his confidante might have—if you *could* have escaped the scrutiny of he who attends the only entrance on the rue du Commandant Schloesing. The toilettes are too obvious, so you would have had to hide the kids and hoped to pass at a particular moment of distraction. But it is only a short walk and you are, except for a groundskeeper or two, quite alone—most surely in November when the wet weather has sent the city in. So if you had taken the path quickly up to avenue Chauvet to the grave of the publisher Hippolyte Marinoni and made a hard right straight almost to the wall of the Place du Trocadéro with the Eiffel Tower looming up, you'd have found many a pretty spot to have dropped your packages one two three, and walking fast along the way past *The Madwoman of Chaillot*, turned right at the alley between the 9th division and the tenth and turned again where the tenth splits and split yourselves quick.

But Nick and his confidantes evidently didn't want to chance the attendants attendance to your entrance and exit, and then, there being those who drop and those who collect and carry off, there would have been far too many exits and entrances to take a chance. The relative emptiness of Passy could not make up for the simple access to Montparnasse.

*   *
*

But you did not return. Never and ever amen. And I, awakening, eventually stood and even walked. Back in my little hotel room (in my absence completely ransacked), I wondered what you had expected to find since you had already relieved me of my wallet and witnessed what was left of my expense account? My wardrobe clearly could not have engaged the interest of even Boudou or some other Paris tramp. I fell into bed to await the sun.

The sun slept in that day, and I, desperate for a little time to heal, did too. Until noon. I knew you would wait until just before the closing hour of 4:00 (darkness already would be swallowing up the place). But I had a lot to accomplish. You gave me no choice—without money, without documents except the one or two I'd put in the hotel deposit box—I had to contact the police, explaining to them in my halting French what was about to happen, where it would, and who might be the participants. I got impatient with their repetitous questions of seeming disinterestedness, and accordingly, shuffling me about until finally the head of the Bureau of drugs took up my case.

What do you expect us to do, sir? he spoke, in English.

Stop the transaction.

But what proof have you this might take place?

198

I had none. But they must, you see, quickly acquire a very great sum, and the dealer will award them only a small percentage for their take. The infants are their only true asset, and should bring a small fortune if sold to the right American or British folks.

But, sir, this is pure speculation. We have only a small force, we are not (I could see it coming) armed with a legion like John Wayne.

They are my children!

The policeman looked back to his desk. Pardon sir, you have told me this, but do you have evidence?

I have a certificate of marriage.

No one is asking you to prove your marriage, sir. We ask simply for a proof of drugs.

No! But I must convince someone, please!

I was your last hope. It appears you have used everyone up.

I turned, despondently, to go away.

Monsieur, I will send one man with you late this afternoon. If there are no arrests, I may jail you.

I hope you don't have to do that.

For the sake of your children, I hope we must.

Yes, I said, in terror and anticipation.

Doubt immediately set in. What had I been saying, thinking, imagining? To have created an event and a place for it to happen in on nothing but a hunch! And the time too! What if, in some discreet hotel, the exchange had already transpired—the young American or British couple having been gently ushered in to see the swathing babes, and after goo-goo eyes and kisses, brought into the parlor for a brief conversation, capped with a packet of cash (opened, in the other room by Nick and counted quick) and the couple to nursery returned, where…suddenly I was sure! The couple, any couple cannot in broad daylight carry two children off without their own fears of being observed let alone those of the captors, and two such encounters would have been beyond Nick's and Leon's quotient of patience. Nope.

It was a drop—just like dope. Somebody else was going to sell them off. I was right. I breathed deeply. I was right. Wasn't I?

At 3:00 I met the Paris policeman, Sergeant Baton (my private nickname for the Monsieur Paul de Horace Lannes of arrondisement Quatorze, detective especialmente de drugs). He did indeed carry a big baton—not as British bully bats against his belly, but where it belongs, neatly tucked into the center of his pants. And while we waited at the sepulchre of families Livet et Carthery he demonstrated how to use it properly.

If you believe *that* story you will doubtlessly believe everything I've written—or absolutely no word of it.

But to return to the subject at hand, or perhaps I should say left behind, Baton was a particularly handsome man of the cloth, sergeant hat and bat. But in actuality we were dressed as cemetery workers, clothed all in green plastic suits, and stood a ways from the families Livet et Cathery, where I had determined was the most likely spot. There are several large sepulchres in that corner, shaded (in summer at least) by two large, gnarled chestnuts. The avenues are bordered

201

on the west and north there by several tombs, most facing west out into the open path. But the families Livet et Carthery face north, with their only other entrance a high ledge fenced from the east. The unclosed tomb easy to access, but difficult to see into from the nearby tower or even from the apartments towering higher yet to the south. We waited with poised rakes or *were* poised rakes—I could no longer remember what was what, which was which. The light was dim when they came across (*you* were not *you* anymore, but one of *them*—the monsters you were with), a tableau of Hannah, Liz, and Leon too, to make certain, I suppose, that they—the other two—did what they had been told. And the infants, clinging to their breasts, were strangely quiet in the cold air of almost night. Leon dropped the bundle, and each of other two quickly kissed the slightly larger bundles they had held and laid them next. In the little light left I could see the three: the bundle of death wrapped in a diaper and wrapped also in a diaper and swaddling cap aside the two slightly squirming diapered and similarly capped bundles of life. The three walking dead figures swerved off. An older man and a very thin girl as quickly appeared, walked up the little stairway to the tomb of the families Livet et Carthery, dating back to 1878, picked up those treasures and, hurriedly passing the familes Peters, Bergeotte-Roy and LaFourcade, were also about to leave in the other direction when two other men suddenly blocked their path. Monsieur Paul de Horace Lannes touched my wrist and as suddenly went forward, blocking the two between the phalanx. One of the other policemen had already spoken and held in his hand a gun. Sergeant Baton took out his too; I went to the woman, relieving her of the *enfants* she now grappled with in opposite hands. The children were squalling something awful. But now at least I could assure them in baby talk. So the captain had sent reinforcements. I had been believed. Had the monster been picked up? I doubted that. For to have been believed is not to say that one is believed *in*. And those before us—the old man and thin girl with wet, black hair—were not monsters, but stupid understudies to the grand nefarious act.

Nick would have been awaiting nearby, on boulevard Edgar Quintet perhaps, for the money to fall upon his lap. When it did not arrive as scheduled, we would certainly have simply stood up and gone off.

*   *
*

O Hannah, Hannah, Hannah! How could you have done that dreadful act? *That* was evil. I know it was. No explanation can alter the fact. Yet I like at least to imagine that Leon had threatened both your lives or that, quick-thinking gal you've always been, you suggested it to spare yourselves the conclusion I had come to.

Yet, I know there would have been no way to bring Leon to desist once he had commenced on that path. Blind passion was not part of this. I don't even want to admit what I know I must. It was planned, from the very beginning a plot. Instead of the abortions you had undergone at least once—perhaps many times previously—you were going to bear these children as Eve must have to Adam the fruit—as something you could merchandise. Instead of a *sou* she had only a soul to sell, while you who already had sold your souls, had simply your innocents left. What did it feel like? What did you think with your lips to their cheeks? Did you fear for them—for yourselves at least—fear for your frivolous days ahead? Or had you managed already to empty your heads as you so clearly had your hearts?

It was hard to convince the Captain that these were my kids. I had only the certificate of marriage and an Hanusse passport—no money, no clothes, no address.

204

Your mother was the only person in the US left to whom I might supplicate. Fortunately, with the differences in language, I could explain the facts of children without filling in all the events. There were children—they were taken—they were tracked—and I now held them (at the moment they were in custody of a city supported nurse). I needed money to bring them back. She was elated with visions of grandmotherhood, of bringing her daughter, through the children's embrace, back into time and space, as if the grave would, so to speak, spill out some of the life it had so sourly swallowed up. Had she known the actual sequence of events I am certain she might have slammed the graveslab down again fast. But in her grandmotherly illusion, she confirmed to the translator and to the capitain that I was—who I was—the father, son-in-law, and wholly gross. Money was sent and received, tickets ordered up, documents stamped, flights confirmed. And I, with the two, Ford and Minnie, flew off in a direction opposite to those so open arms.

Come back!!

*   *
*

I did. Come back. To where no one was waiting for me, for us. Poor Hanusse. Poor us. For yes, we could stay here and be here always—at a cost of near complete isolation. But it does not seem that today as the topless hula girls sway across the Pais du Port'it, all hips hugged in green plastic strips. The boat is in. The sailors still on sea legs, sway in time to their tuneless trance. We were Circe, are still today.

Shadows are swallowing us up as well. The British have all gone in and won't be out again until 8:00. And although the processions continue to pass, there is, in their tone and pace, a pause, before things will later move into a long and gradually expanding bacchanal. Some Russian boys are back, having left their buddies to enjoy what they first had their fill of. They must be the alpha males of the mates, the chosen ones of Darwin's plot. I look them over carefully. They are beautiful, but I, still in tears, fear to think of my daughter lying in that bed. Is there enjoyment there or simply terror. She is, I am certain, scared, despite the V-inspired little lesson of feminine flirtation I formerly observed.

I smoke a cigarette. I love her so!

O Hannah, how could you have let her go? When need was all she had? She now, at least, has survival on her side—and spirit, she has that. And now it is my turn to lay her in the sepulchre of a nature so terribly unsure. One of three, seeing me staring so intently at them, winks. I simply smile, toast them through the air. He toasts back. I can no longer tell the difference between what invites and what mocks.

I am getting too old I guess, as I write.

ACT III

Time passes.

ACT IV

See, I am such a sentimentalist! An imitator! Just a hack. I now see that one of Russian sailors has a small scratch on his cheek. He must be Alpha 1, Alexander I shall call him, after the great St. Petersburg prospekt. Yes, she has spirit. She will be all right.

The Russian Boris—not Alexander—or perhaps even Dimitri, winks once more. What does it mean? I stare more intently into his eyes. They are gentle. I hope the child is his.

I need a bathroom and, as I look toward our public accommodations—basically just a dark trench in an shed—his eyes follow mine. As I stand, so does he, and at the trench he is already there, erect. We kiss, a most exciting kiss. And just as suddenly he is down on his knees. I am pleased. He stands as I bend and then the same cock that has just a hour or two before (maybe three) hurt my little girl so much is, with excruciating pain, shoved into my ass. The excitement is complete, but he, very slowly, extrudes, enters, extrudes, enters, extrudes, enters—my butt is all bloody now. In exhaustion, I pull up my pants.

I don't how to say this, but that was the most important fuck—and the very best—I have received. Within those brief seconds of ecstasy, I was able to release Minnie to her own destiny. Every father needs a good fuck to make him realize he has been an ass all of his life.

The Russians have disappeared again.

O Hannah, your disapprobation doesn't impress me in the least. Can you think that if the word has gotten out about our available adolescents, that the world doesn't know about our other sexual eccentricities, that the news hasn't spread across the planet. With foreigners it's always open season. In Hanusse we take what we can get.

*   *
    *

Upon his release from prison, Wilde had no choice but to take up residence in France. In 1895, howevever, Lord Alfred Douglas, Oscar's beloved Bosie, entreated him to take up residence with him in Naples. Wilde surely knew what that would mean: he would be even further ostracized. But with Bosie's assurance to take care of him and given the refusal of Oscar's wife to see him, he had little choice. His friends in Paris, Reggie Turner and others, had turned down his monetary requests. Most importantly, he still loved the boy, had given nearly everything up for his sake.

Near the end of September, the couple moved into the Villa Giudice in the wealthy quarter of Posillipo, to

Naples' north. Almost immediately the letters of shock and dismay poured in. Constance, Wilde's wife, threatened to cut his small £25 weekly allowance. Lady Queensbury threatened to cut her sizeably larger support of her son. But she was even crueller in her machinations to separate the two: she would offer to pay Douglas's debts and pay Wilde £200 if both signed an agreement never to live again under the same roof.

Despite protestations from both Wilde and Douglas, they recognized that, without someone's intervention, they must separate. No interventions were forthcoming, and, not without some rancour, Wilde released Douglas from his agreement to spend the rest of their lives together.

On December 3rd Douglas left. Wilde stayed on in Naples for a while, his public appearances accompanied by the many slights, sniggers, and sneers he would have to endure for the rest of his years. He accompanied an acquaintance to meet Baron von Gloeden, the photographer, in Taormina, but otherwise spent his days in Neapolitan cafés, awarding his company to anyone willing to pay for one or two drinks.

In February he returned to Paris, where, except for brief trips, he was to remain ensconced in the Hôtel d'Alsace

*on the rue des Beaux-Arts for the rest of his life. Wilde
had a few joyful moments there, such as the publication
of his* The Ballad of Reading Goal *under the name C.3.3.
It was a success, but he saw no money from it.*

*Mostly these days were spent drinking the deadly com-
bination of brandy and absinthe. Occasionally he was
seen with a young man on his arm, which brought clucks
of disapproval even from the sexually tolerant Paris press.
But his most controversial companion was of a political
rather than sexual* scandale. *Soon after his arrival in
Paris Wilde befriended the Commandant Ferdinand
Walsin-Esterhazy—the man who had committed the
actual spying for which Alfred Dreyfus was accused and
imprisoned. Zola, Wilde's former friend, had written*
J'Accuse *on the 13th of January 1898, and in February
was convicted of libel and sentenced to imprisonment.*

*But even Esterhazy's admission in Wilde's company that
he had indeed committed the treacherous acts did not
dissuade Wilde that his company was entertaining: "It's
always a mistake to be innocent," quipped Wilde. "To be
a criminal takes imagination and courage." Zola escaped
to England; Wilde was left these last days without a route
of retreat.*

The slights, sneers, and sniggers continued. And Wilde gradually lost the will to live, remaining for longer and longer periods of time in bed. Whistler was silent upon his encounter with Wilde in a restaurant and later commented to others: "Wilde is working on The Bugger's Opera." *Wilde fled from even the few intimacies proffered him.*

For several months now he had been suffering from a severe rash which he called his "mussel poisoning," and which the doctors diagnosed as neurasthenia. But his final illness began in the ear. A small operation was performed in his room, but over a period of weeks in October, his ear developed an abscess, which, in turn, led to meningitis. It was now apparent that this infection was related to the syphilis he had contracted at the age of twenty. For a short while, Wilde retained his sense of humor—"My wallpaper and I are fighting a dual to the death. One of us has to go."—but he soon begin to mix his words, asking for paraffin *when he meant the newspaper* Patrie.

His friends Robert Ross and Reginald Turner took turns in watching over him. On the 29th of November 1900, Ross sent for a Catholic priest, and through hand signals Wilde approved his last rites. He was 45.

212

At 5:30 AM the next morning, Ross and Turner experienced the terrifying aural performance of Wilde's death rattle, sounding like the "turning of a crank." Blood and foam issued from his mouth. Upon his death his body emanated fluids from each and every orifice.

On December 2nd, in an inexpensive coffin and a hearse bearing the numeral 13, Wilde was taken from  *St. Germain-des-Prés to the cemetery at Bagneau. In 1909, Wilde's remains were moved from Bagneau to Père Lachaise.*

[SOURCE: Richard Ellmann, *Oscar Wilde* (London: Penguin, 1988; first published London: Hamish Hamilton, 1987).]

*

When we were very young Leon once admitted to me that he preferred women to men. Their bodies are made for each other, he said. It is a natural marriage of form

213

and contentment. But being with men, he added, I find more exciting, more thrilling as a sexual event. If ever it becomes acceptable to be a homosexual I am certain there will be far fewer of them.

Leon was always full of shit, speaking as if what he said really meant something insightful and profound. For whatever you say, Leon was not gay. He was just completely interested in change. In his logic, if something was societally wrong, it was something one simply had to experience, quick—and over and over again. A lot of tourists think that is the way it is with us. That we in Hanusse are just wonderfully tolerant, believers in a sort of Aegean polygamousness similar to the Pacific pacifism of the Tahitians. But they do not comprehend. Our sexual openness is as socially orchestrated as the Puritan ethics of a Connecticutian. We are utterly committed to fraternizing with foreign folk. It is not a whim or want of will or lackadaisical lust. It is an utter devotion not just to keep the tourists coming back to and in us, but a belief deeply inbred. A stranger simply must be taken to bed—or barn or bathroom or even bush; it's a necessity, however nice.

So what I just did was not what you might have read it as: an attempt to retain sexual power over my daughter through some dupe's dripping cock come directly from her cunt. For with us there is no taboo attached, and accordingly, no salaciousness connected with the act. Pleasure is a principle, not a pasttime.

I am "gay" because I want to be, not because my mommy mistreated me or my daddy left with the babysitter on his back. I like homosexual acts—nearly every one, except those involving torture and unbearable pain. And sex with women—although not encouraged in this society—is the same. A boy is beautiful to put a cock into. It is a simple as that.

But as we know, *that* is never simple—although it should be, could be, might. Evil is….? For many, everything I've written you, in these letters, this little play for your attention. For you know, as well as I do, the villain is still on the loose—whether it be Leon or me. And I am terrified of that encounter for fear of what I will find out!

How could they let him free after what he has done? For, although he lost you, he would not lose me. The simpleton had, afterall, become a challenge, a test of his empty philosophy. In his virile attractiveness and ability to entrance, Leon was used to being listened to, to having his way about things. But the shrimp had cut their fisherman's net, a dangerous precedent. I was supposed to be dead. And I was in a land of enchanters, on account of it, beyond compare. Perhaps he had always seen that in me, that part of my inheritance I had attempted to hide, but which flashed occasionally in my eyes, in my body bending in the night, keeping a tiny distance from himself. Now it was time to draw the line in. The old man and the sea played out in a version soap opera upon TV.

I am afraid of my encounter again with him. You can understand if I keep postponing the eventuality of it.

*

William Tell *was a great success in its 1829 premiere. It was proclaimed by the Paris press as Rossini's masterpiece, and received over 500 performances in the French capital during the author's life.*

But over the next few years, ill health plagued him. On a recuperative trip to Aix-les-Bains in 1830 the composer met the legendary courtesan Olympe Pelissier, who, at 35, had already had affairs with Honoré Balzac, Eugène Sue, and the painter Horace Vernet. Olympe returned with Rossini to Paris as his mistress and, ultimately, his nurse.

From 1834–1855, Rossini spent his time in Bologna, Milan, and Florence, making only brief returns to Paris. But with continued hydrophobia, an infection to his urinary system, and extreme neurasthenia—brought on, most likely from venereal disease—Rossini was convinced by Olympe that they must return to Paris, now ruled by Napolean III. There he was visited by friends and distinguished colleagues such as Richard Wagner, who in 1860 payed a visit to the master. Wagner praised Guillaume Tell, *describing it as a "music for all times."*

During the next eight years, despite frail health and intense pain, Rossini continued to participate in the contemporary music scene, holding regular Saturday soirées. But recently Rossini had developed cancer of the rectum, and in November 1868 was operated on in Passy. His recovery was brief, and with the onset of death, Olympe persuaded him to receive the Last Sacrament. On Friday the 13th, he died. Gustave

Doré was called in to sketch the composer on his death-bed; and Rossini's coffin was taken for his burial in Père Lachaise.

His body was moved to Florence in 1887, where in 1912 a tomb was erected over it. His tomb in Paris remains empty.

[SOURCE: Nicholas Till, *Rossini: His Life and Times* (New York: Hippocrene Books, 1983).]

*

On March 15, 1841, after six months of migraines, Marie-Henri Beyle had a stroke in Italy near Civitavecchia. Suddenly he forgot all his French, and could not even ask for a glass of water. After eight or ten minutes, his memory came back, but he remained quite exhausted. In the year previous Beyle, better know as Stendhal, had had four such losses of memory. Just ten days earlier he had been unable to find the word for "glass."

In the weeks following the Consul continued to feel a tremendous tiredness come over him. In July a young woman, Mme Francois Bouchot, daughter to the celebrated singer, came to Civitavecchia to swim. Beyle sought her out sexually. But over the next few months it

218

was clear that his health had begun to disintegrate. In November he returned to Paris, eventually settling at 78 rue de Petits-Champs.

Either in late February or early March 1842, Beyle had another stroke, which left him partly paralyzed. In mid-March, however, he seemed better, promising through contract to deliver a monthly story to the Revue des Deux Mondes.

On the evening of March 22nd, he suffered a stroke on the rue Neuvre-des-capucines, near the entrance to the Ministry of Foreign Affairs. The previous April he had written: "I think there is nothing ridiculous in dying in the street, when you don't do it on purpose." He died the next morning, and was buried at the Cimetière Montmartre. In 1962 his  *tomb was moved to a site apart from the railway viaduct under which he had originally lain.*

[SOURCE: Joanna Richardson, *Stendhal* (London: Victor Gollancz, 1974).]

*

On November 29th, 1841, Henri Beyle attended the premiere of La Chaîne, *the most recent comedy of Eugène Scribe, a playwright, whom he had earlier castigated for his commercialism, but whose newest play "delighted" him.*

Over the next few years, as scores of Scribe's plays continued to dominate French theater, younger writers and journalists began to attack the popular playwright. In 1855 two Paris papers actually charged him with causing Gérard de Nerval's suicide, since Nerval's play had been declined by the Théatre Royal, which had selected Scribe's Le Vieux Château *instead.*

Scribe sued for libel, and won. The journalist, Philippe Audébrand, and the publisher were sentenced to three months in prison. Ruined and disgraced, the publisher sold his paper to Le Figaro.

Scribe's pen lessened in its flow, but he continued publishing plays for another six years. On the evening of February 20th, 1861, Scribe met with the new president

220

of the Société des Auteurs et Compositeurs Drama- tiques. He left his host's home in seemingly good health, but was found by his servant upon his ar- rival home dead in his car- riage. Thousands stood through the rain to witness his burial in Père Lachaise.

*

The parades have once again picked up. A chorus of boys in tight shorts are herded together by a priest singing a sprintly religious prayer, to which they are the answer apparently. The Russian boys—all them at once—have returned to their favorite haunt, *sans* Minnie (where have they left her? Again, I am nervous!) Even the British are back!

Now for the acrobats! They dive into a flip and a sud- den, almost unseen stand, before they flip and repeat. It is a feat we would all wish we could achieve. And some boys on the fringe are trying, in clumsy imita- tion, actually to succeed. I check for Ford among them.

He is not there. And where is V?

The little girls arrive in twenty donkey carts. They are dressed all in white, of which even the Russians, whose eyes have gotten wide, know the meaning. Dimitri and his friends tip their chairs back as if to evidence—obviously to themselves—their disinterest. And as soon I see Minnie with two other girls her age join them. I sigh. In their dissatisfaction she will stay safe. Alexander puts his arm around and Dimitri winks at me again. Minnie suddenly recognizes the figure of her father and waves to make the men more jealous. Alexander brings her closer and Dimitri frowns in suspicion until she leans into his ear to whisper, obviously, "That is my papa!" At first the eyebrows rise—he is a bit distressed—but then the recognition and the inevitable hearty laugh. He will say nothing now, nothing to my Minnie or his mates. But he has suddenly a legend to tell for his entire life. He is satisfied, leans back, and expanding his chest in secret pride, actually grows fat.

I can see him, twenty years from this instant—O it is so frightening!—as he sits, belly bulging by his fireplace—or an entire world of entertainment, computer, television, motion picture, video, and CD transmogrified into space—with his grandchildren at his knee speaking somewhat censoriously, there was a time (O yes he was once young!)—he fucked a young virgin and upon finishing fucked—this was years ago—her father. "In Hanusse they are very loose," so the old saying goes. But she had terrifically tight tits.

They won't have heard a word of it.

*

The year 1869 began badly, with a near-fatal accident, and got worse for the Brothers Goncourt. Jules, in particular, was terribly sensitive to noise. Their house in Anteuil had a neighbor with a stable and three very loud little girls. They escaped to the Grand Hôtel in Passy, and later to a hotel generally occupied by traveling salesmen. But these also proved impossible, and, upon Jules suffering a liver attack, they traveled to the mineral and ferruginous baths of Royate, a "region of gloom," filled with folks suffering from skin rashes, nerves, hysteria, and paralysis. Various other locales were just as insufferably noisy. Swarming brats, the bells of Catholic churches, grated on the ears of the brothers, desperate in their isolation and increasing neglect to continue their writing.

1870 was no better. Again there were visits to the baths, while Jules' nervous condition appeared to increase. Depression set in more often, and, despite his persistent attempts to work on their current project, his intelligence was fading. He mispronounced r and s, which at times made his talk seem that of a child's. He lost interest in nearly everything but nature, and forgot even how to spell the artist Watteau's name.

There were times when Edmond nearly grew violent, grabbing his brother by the collar as if to choke. The look in his brother's eyes made him weep. In a letter to Flaubert he admitted of suicidal thoughts. His brother became his child.

One by one, they returned to their beloved locations of the past: Bas-Meudon, Saint-Cloud. There was no silence anywhere to be found. In May Jules, reading over a name and attempting to repeat it, could not say it out. His agitation brought his brother to despair. In June, still reading a novel he had committed to finish, he stumbled and fell into a chair. Inarticulate sounds, loud laughter, and a hoarse cry followed before the onset of delirium. Visions plagued him for the remainder of the day. The brain had disintegrated at its base reported the doctor the following morning. Jules survived for five days *longer. On Sunday he cried out, turned yellow, and, his eyes wet with tears, he fell into death.*

Along the procession from church to the cemetery at Montmartre, Edmond seemed to age, his hair literally turning white in the very course. Upon returning to their home in Anteuil, Edmond laid portraits of his brother upon his bedclothes, gazing upon them until all turned dark. "It was the intensity of his art, the focus of a undistracted brain upon all the subtleties of language, the complete preoccupation with a literary life, that resulted in the brain's disintegration," wrote Edmond to Théophile Gautier. Had he not read his brother's 1864 entry, ponders the Goncourt's biographer André Billy, in which Jules admits to having contracted syphilis?

The "widow," as Edmond's friends mockingly referred to him, lived on for 31 years. His later career was not a distinguished one, and he admitted to dreaming every night, for a great time, of his brother.

His close friendship with the Daudets was often a strained one, in the past because of Mme. Daudet's emotional feeling for him, which may have bordered on love, but often expressed itself in a fierce protection of her husband, Alphonse. Edmond attributed Daudet's occasional

225

outbursts to a brain haunted by morphia; but, in fact, it had often to do with petty literary bickerings, particularly centered on membership in the French Academy. Goncourt was resolute in setting up, in accordance with Jules' desires, a new Goncourt *academy*. And he had, in his will, left Daudet to be its executor. His fear was that his friend desired to be accepted by, and, if invited, would quickly become a member of the Academie Française. Mme. Daudet certainly would have pushed her husband in that direction. She, moreover, was quite annoyed with Edmond for allowing his *Journal* to be published in L'Echo de Paris, since they had only recently lampooned Léon, her son.

But in July things were patched up, and Edmond left the gare de Lyon on a visit to the Daudet's in Champrosay. The first few nights were spent in friendly and nostalgic discussions, the two authors recalling their dinners with Flaubert, Zola, and Turgenev.

Edmond had complained upon arriving of a very dry tongue, and on the second day of his visit complained again of being thirsty. The third day also he could not eat. He slept badly at night. The following day he decided to remain only on milk, and prepared for his bath, which at Champrosay was across the yard. Daudet found

him an hour later, lying, half-dressed, across the bed,
without the energy to crawl beneath the sheets. Edmond's
right side ached and his teeth were chattering with chill.

That evening Mme. Daudet found him quivering in his
bed. A doctor was called. He diagnosed congestion of the
lungs. Mustard plasters, injections of caffeine, and ether
were administered. But the patient remained "So
tired....so tired."

A new doctor was sent for, and upon his arrival the
Daudets retired. In the middle of the night the doctor
called for Alphonse and his wife: the patient was dying.
They attempted to speak to him, but in a short while he
was dead.

Mme. Daudet ordered roses cut from her garden to adorn
Edmond's room and bed.

At least one correspondent, however, wondered why, in a
day when "even old men can be cured of congestion,"
Edmond had died so quickly. Why had the Daudets not sat
up with him, had they treated his servant girls who arrived
on the scene the next morning so rudely, and had they
discussed before them their desire not to be held respon-
sible for the contents of the money on Edmond's person.

 *Zola, who himself had been at odds with both the Daudets and E d m o n d (only a few months earlier Edmond had written of the Zola home: "Ah, that house, where there is never the joy of putting a little flame on the hearth."), spoke eloquently at the Goncourts' graveside in Montmartre.*

[SOURCE: André Billy, *The Goncourt Brothers,* trans. by Margaret Shaw. (London: A. Deutsch, 1960).]

*   *
*

ACT III

Time passes again.

ACT IV

In the Paris of 1943 the major occupation of most of its inhabitants was keeping warm. Jean Giraudoux was no exception.

His most recent play, Sodom and Gomorrah, *which opened in October, was a bleak one, in which men and women joined their gender for the doom that awaited them. He had just completed the more hopeful and optimistic comedy,* The Madwoman of Chaillot, *but even the playwright could not imagine its production until 1945.*

In a small hotel on rue Cambon, Giraudoux took up residence with his dog Puck. He was cold, but continued to write. At Christmas he was ill with influenza, and was unable to attend his play's performance.

With the New Year he felt better, but towards the end of the month his flu re-

turned, and acute uremia set in. A meningeal hemor-
rhage followed. Three days of suffering left him exhausted,
and he died on the morning of January 31st. He was bur-
ied in the far right corner, opposite the entrance, of the
small cemetery in Passy, near the graves of the author
Nathalie Barney, Princes Georges Branson and Dimitri
Galitzine, and Princesses Sophie de Hoheng-dolseck and
Guilaíme de Monaco, over which the Eiffel Tower looms.

[SOURCE: Donald Inskip, *Jean Giraudoux: The Making of a Drama-*
tist (London: Oxford University Press, 1958).]

*

Simone de Beauvoir was quite upset. Sartre had long been
ill, and now he began to confuse things linguistically. When
Arlette told him that she had been to a special screening
of a Lanzmann film, he interrupted to tell her that she
had not been the only one to attend, "Arlette went too."

His handwriting had grown illegible. And now, in a se-
ries of interviews with Benny Lévy, Sartre quarrelled with
his earlier self, disavowing important tenants of his phi-
losophy. Lévy diminished Sartre's ideas of realitivity. His
ideas on history were presented as a sort of messianic con-
ception of ethics. Simone was more than upset, she was
shocked.

230

On March 19th, 1980, just after the publication of the second installment of the interviews in Les Temps modernes, *Simone found Sartre sitting on the edge of his bed, gasping for breath. The attack had begun four hours before, but he had been too weak to reach the door of her bedroom. Because of an unpaid bill, the telephone was disconnected. She ran to a neighbor's apartment, and made the call for the ambulance. With oxygen mask over his face, Sartre was wheeled into intensive care at Broussais.*

Journalists disguised as nurses unsuccessfully attempted to sneak into his room. The photograph of a sleeping Sartre in his hospital bed, printed in Match, *was obtained from a rooftop across the way.*

In a delirium brought on by a high fever, Sartre lay, an arterial blockage preventing him from getting proper circulation. His kidneys were too weak to function, and his bedsores had become gangrenous.

Arlette spent the mornings with him, Simone the afternoons. "How will we pay for the funeral" he asked de Beauvoir. The next day he took her wrist and spoke: "I love you very much my dear Beaver."

By April 14th, he fell into a coma. His friends gathered. Sartre died the next day. De Beauvoir asked to be left alone with him and lay down next to him beneath the sheet. Warned by a nurse of the dangers of gangrene, she  *lay atop the bedding and slept.*

On the 19th of April Sartre was buried in Cimitière du Montparnasse, with over 50,000 people following the hearse. De Beauvoir, who had taken a heavy dose of valium, could hardly see the hundreds of people with their cameras. Friends surrounded her with joined hands to protect her privacy.

The site was so crowded that some spectators were knocked to the ground, one man falling into the open grave.

Six years later Simone was buried in the same plot.

[SOURCE: Ronald Hayman, *Writing Against: A Biography of Sartre* (London: Weidenfeld and Nicolson, 1986).]

*

I *am* mad! There is no excuse for my continuation.
Black out! END OF PLAY.

Forgive me father for I have sinned. Forgive me father for I have sinned—even if I don't feel I have. Forgive me father….. [I whisper in the dark.]

Forgive me futher for I have sense. Forgive me farther for I have *sans. Rien.* Where is Ford?

Forgive me pappa! For me pappa! Forgive me pappa!

*

In his *Macquette of History* Claude Ricochet writes: "History does not exist. Like a great, great grandfather, it lies rotten in its crypt. Only through bits and pieces of memory, story-telling, exaggeration, lies and forgetfulness do we the living create it, make it up, and in this we know, instinctively, history has nothing at all to do with Facts, with the truth of our existence. It is a pile of rubbish each of us sorts through to figure out what might be saved.

This fact saddens us. It would be easier to have learned from the past, to discover how not to repeat the terrible stupidities, atrocities, the general foolishness of the human race. If history could exist, how we might learn from it! But we know, inwardly we know, the moment it becomes history, it becomes something no longer connected with the truth we seek within each moment of our day. We are left with threads, old remnants that we try to weave together without success.

Imagine if history did exist, if it could live along with us, as a breathing force. How heavy it would weigh. So many dead heaping up reality upon so few living left. We could only suffocate.

All the more important that, ineffectual as we are, we attempt to resew the pattern over and again. Like Penelope, we must weave to unwind and weave once more, each time ever so slightly varing the design—until, as we are about to fall into our own burial plots, we have created something completely different from what we thought at the beginning we might create. As in the child's game of telephone, we have repeated the words so many times that we, each of us alone and each of us as a part of generation, have utterly transformed the message. What might once have been feared is now revered, the sacred is at last profane."

*

In his *Apologies* he adds: "The dead—those whom the whole civilization is so eager to forget—are more powerful than kings, queens, premiers and presidents. It is

235

terrible the stories they tell, over and over again. As the living it is essential, absolutely essential that we refuse to listen to them. For life is, through their voices, eternally a tale of woe. The most frightening of them are the cheeful ones, in fact. For we know, as the living do naturally, that what they thought was so important, what they fought for their entire lives, believed in, died for perhaps, has absolutely no real meaning for us. If it had, we would collapse, be truly hollow for what we know its life's absolute emptiness. Time does not heal wounds, it wounds all heels, turns back to snap at and ultimately swallow up everyone in its tracks."

*

The French love to talk. Even an exasperated shrug becomes *Ah oooh lá lá lá lá!* So one must take everything a Frenchman says with a grain of salt. However, because they talk, unlike the Hanussee—who simply stand, smile, wave, wink—and the Americans—who either keep everything close to their chests or have to get everything off—or the British—who babble or who say nothing at all whatsoever—or the Indians—who have nothing at all to say but say it nonetheless very very very fast—and the Italians—who use their fingers and hands, after their eyes, breasts, behinds and in-betweens have so elegantly expressed it, to say what is

236

left—and the Spaniards—who protest what they say before they say it and debate it while it's being said—and the Australians—who speak argot and think of it as thought—the French saying something about everything is, when compared with a grain of salt, a shinning pillar of a lot.

So I believe it more than most. I met Ricochet, you know, in those terrible Paris days. Most of the time was spent trying to find Leon's whereabouts, but at nights, Paris nights! I heard that Ricochet was showing one of his films with a lecture to follow. Someone—it must have been George Reimat (you remember him? the gay liberation leader at Queen's College, the one who put the "Queens" in Queens, according to his political slogan)—who, knowing only the most archane of motion pictures, told me Ricochet was gay—and a theorist to boot. A gay theorist-cinematographer fascinated me: I couldn't comprehend what that might mean. Gay poets, Ginsburg, O'Hara, Ashbery, I could assimilate, but film and theory are such social things with disciples and an entire entourage.

In those days, however, Ricochet wasn't a celebrity yet, and he had not retreated to the caves with sexually celibate monks. He was just a man who was showing a very strange and difficult movie to grasp. I've never seen anything like that film before or since.

The actors were simply his friends, filmed over several evenings in his and their apartments or places of employment. Some just sat at a table or on a couch and spoke about friends, feelings, of their discomfort at being photographed. Some were all camp, others utterly serious—but even they with a great deal of humor. Others preferred to play out their lives with performances in bed.

Ricochet overlaid the talk with images of sex, and the bed-bound activity with nearly endless talk. The result—in those days—was utterly innovative and a bit of a shock. There was one figure, Monsieur B- I think he was called, who worked as a bartender nights in a bar for working class men. He was beautiful, tall, lean, with big brown eyes and long black eyelashes, endowed, without any doubt, with a long, narrow, uncut cock. He stood, hour after hour over his patrons, workers, a few almost as attractive as he, but quite obviously married and straight. He spoke softly about their lives, poured beer into their glasses, lit their cigarettes. But he had always afterwards to immediately back away a bit. His major activity, except for the mixing and pouring of drinks, was to clean. And clean he did, not only the bar, glasses, bottles, ash trays and mirror to his back, but pictures, portraits, doors, clocks—all so sincerely and sensually that when he returned to pour a drink or occasionally to light up a customer's fag, it was a totally erotic act. Many of times the eyes of the server and receiver met, but both turned attentions elsewhere at once, while the thin long fingers of the attendant busy in the art of pouring wine or putting a glass of beer before (while utterly ignored) spoke an entire encyclopedia of sex.

During and opposed to this, Ricochet had recorded over the voice of a very angry and betrayed transvestite, carping, caviling, completely camp. The result was the most painful segment of cinema I have ever experienced. The careful hug of the glass of kir against the music of a careless castigation of what in those days we described as a tired old queen was devastating. And when, at the end, the beautiful man put on his leather coat and it became apparent all at once that he was the lover of the most surly and obnoxious of that bar's drunks, the shrill inflection of the queen was, after all, absolutely justified.

I went home with that man in the film, for the bartender had been played by Ricochet himself. In the theater there had been only four patrons. The lecture did not take place.

When I returned to Hanusse I wrote to explain my lack of words that night. He never corresponded, but sent me his books until his death. You see I was right: the personal was transformed into the public; what he had to say to me was the same he said to everyone. The secrets of the philosopher are the philosophy itself. And in the film that was, as well, what he had done: publicly scrutinized his own and his friends' private lives.

You know, he really had worked as a bartend.

*

Proust found it ludicrous "to be dying incessantly without achieving death," but his mild heart attacks had gotten worse, and for days at a time he lay in his overheated bedroom. He often, when out walking, could not remember certain words or names. On other days he simply did not have the energy to get up. For entire weeks he would drink only beer, brought him from the Ritz, or eat only ice cream.

240

André Gide had written a mostly positive review, published just previous to Guermantes, *and Proust suddenly wanted to see Gide once more. Several times he sent a carriage to bring André to him. And in late May 1921, Gide appeared. Gide began discussing homosexuality, but Proust interrupted, asking his guest to explain the gospel teachings. Later in the conversation, Proust argued that Baudelaire, with all of his mention of Lesbos, must have been a homosexual. Gide's demurral was understood as disparagement.*

Upon another visit, Gide argued that Proust seemed to have stigmatized homosexuality in his great work. But, Gide observed, that what we found "ignoble, ridiculous or disgusting, does not to him seem so repulsive." Proust's room, Gide observed, was "a black den." Proust's face was "a waxy mask." Natalie Clifford Barney, upon her visit later that year, thought Proust looked "like a corpse laid out in a coffin."

Proust was now completing Sodom and Gomorrah, *and worked to get review attention for it, encouraging* L'Opinion *to extract Gide's earlier review, and pushed Léon Daudet—who had helped Proust win the Goncourt prize—to publish in the anti-semitic* Le Revue France.

But he was growing weaker, locked away in his overly-heated rooms. Only occasionally did he go out. At a restaurant he had to ask for a bottle of Contrexéville water ten times before the waiter could comprehend. His aphasia had become more serious.

In September he fell in his bedroom, and mistakenly took an overdose of the narcotics opium, Vexonal and Dial. For several weeks he remained in bed with a high fever. Once again, he refused to eat.

In 1922 Proust attended two great balls, one at the de Beaumont's, the second at the Ritz, where he reencountered Paul Morand, with whom he had conceived a love affair five years previous. But he refused most other invitations. At times he felt suicidal, regretting he had no cyanide.

He continued working, nonetheless, on the third and fourth parts of Sodome *(which would later be called* The Prisoner *and* Albertine Gone*); and in the beginning of the Spring, 1922, Proust wrote in his manuscript the words "The End." Now I can die he said to Céleste.*

To celebrate the publication of Sodome, *his friends the Schiffs were giving a dinner party, but in his prepara-*

tions for the event, Proust forgot to dilute his adrenalin and passed out, partly because of pain of the digestive system. He finally was able to see his friends in May at a party at the Ritz for Stravinsky, Diaghilev, Picasso, and a writer just arrived in Paris, James Joyce.

Like many an Irishman, Joyce had more than one story to tell of his and Proust's encounter. The dialectic was either one of headaches (Joyce) and stomach problems (Proust) or duchesses (Proust) and chambermaids (Joyce). Or perhaps, as Joyce told another friend, the great writers talked only of trifles. It may be that Proust repeatedly uttered only one word, "No." The meeting was apparently unmomentous.

Proust's condition was worsening. A visit from Lucien Daudet, the boy with whom Proust had had an affair many years before and over whom Proust had once dueled (and the son of Alphonse and brother to Léon) was a sad one, Lucien recognizing how sick the man was. His attempt to embrace him resulted in Proust's pulling away, "I have not washed or shaved!" His hand was all Proust offered Lucien's lips.

In June Proust contracted rheumatic fever, which kept his temperature at 102 degrees. But by July he was well enough to go with friends to Bœuf sur le toit, the cabaret favored by Cocteau, filled with, as Proust described them, "pimps and queers." As he done so often in the past (usually over anti-Dreyfusian remarks), Proust challenged one man to a duel, who apologized via post the next morning.

Illness continued to plague him. Proust now became convinced that cracks in his chimney were filling his room with carbon monoxide, and the man who had for so long lived in a hot-house environment so intense that visitors often had to leave the room to catch a whiff of fresh air, commanded that his fire no longer be lit. The consequence was influenza.

Proust coughed continuously, but nothing came up. In late October he was warned if he did not change his habits and did not sleep, he would die of pneumonia. His brother, Robert, a doctor himself, also intervened, warning Proust of the consequences. Proust ordered Céleste never to admit him again.

On November 12th the author sent a bouquet of flowers to his doctor and another to Léon Daudet. On November 17th, he asked Céleste "What is going to happen if I cannot manage by myself anymore?" He now had pneumonia and an abscess on the lung.

244

Robert was called, and Proust ordered one of his favorite childhood dishes. Later he canceled it. He was too tired to eat.

At 7:00 the next morning he called for coffee. Proust drank a little, but signaled to be left alone. Céleste left, but remained standing outside the door, holding her breath so as not to be heard. When he rang the bell, Proust complained of the presence of a horrible fat woman dressed in black. Céleste offered to chase her away, but he wanted a better look. When he fell asleep, she called to Dr. Bize and to Robert. His fingers, in their movements of trying to gather in things, had terrified her.

Proust asked for cold beer. The doctor arrived and gave him an injection. "Oh Céleste," he cried out. At half-past four, in the company of Céleste and his brother, Proust closed his eyes in death. Each cut a lock of Proust's hair, the only thing

about him, as Francois Mauriac had observed, that seemed to be alive. Léon Daudet arrived first, and wept. He remained with Céleste through the night. When Paul Morand arrived on Sunday, he told the story how Proust, out of weariness, would often close his eyes, but leave one open, ever so slightly, to watch. He's still doing that. Proust was buried on the 22nd of November in Père Lachaise.

[SOURCE: Ronald Hayman, *Proust: A Biography* (New York: HarperCollins, 1990).]

*

As he turned 60, Hector Berlioz found that life had grown more and more difficult. A few years earlier his first wife, Harriet Smithson, had died, "a formlesss mass of flesh." He recalled how 27 years earlier she had been at the center of the Paris intellectual elite. And just two years earlier, his second wife and former lover, Marie Recio, had died of a sudden heart attack; she had just turned 48. Even her successor to his love, the gentle Amélie, whom he had met in the cemetery, had died, without him knowing it. In 1861 also, Eugéne Scribe, from whom he had unsuccessfuly attempted to get a serious libretto, died; so too did Henri Murger and Chelard, who directed the Weimar chapel and had remained a lifelong friend. And

246

at the very moment when he should have been recognized for his achievements, friends, even his dear Liszt, had gone over instead to the side of what they claimed to be the future of music: the work of Richard Wagner. "Never did I have so many windmills to tilt at as this year," Berlioz had written. "I am surrounded by lunatics." And still no production of his Les Troyens was in sight. When he was not musically involved, he was generally to be found ill in bed.

One of the few joys of the past year had been his reading of Salammbô by Flaubert, and he wrote an enthusiastic letter and a notice in Débats.

More friends died: his close artist friend Eugène Delacroix died in semi-neglect; Alfred Vigny, "godfather, so to speak," of his Benvenuto Cellini, died in obscurity; Léon de Wailly, friend to Vigny and librettist of Cellini died; and his close friend Horace Vernet, whose mistress, Olympe Pelissier, had joined Berlioz's arch-enemy, Rossini.

The 1863 production of Les Troyens presented a mutilated, under-rehearsed, and over-staged version of the work, but it was generally successful, save in the popular pamphlets and news-sheets of the day, which described *the burial of the Trojans at Père Lachaise and confounded Berlioz and Wagner as Beethoven's sons.*

The following year, other friends died. Berlioz felt that his generation had nearly disappeared. Then at age 64, Berlioz heard the terrible news of his his son's death. Louis and he had been extremely close; the boy had been described by his biographer as having "abnormal attachment" to him, and Berlioz described their relationship to contain a love more like that between brothers. Berlioz could no longer sleep, even with heavy doses of laudanum. He walked the streets like a narcotized man. He was sent to take the waters of Néris. Gradually his excellent handwriting gave out and became illegible. Although the handwriting recovered, Berlioz did not. He traveled to Nice, and from there drove to Monte Carlo to climb the rocks. Dizziness ensued, and he fell, bruised and bleeding. The next day in Nice, he attempted to walk, but fell again, and remained after for a week in bed.

Back in Paris, he heard of the deaths of yet more enemies and friends. His friend Ferrard died in September; a fellow student at the Conservatoire, Léon Kreutzer, died in October; and in November Rossini was buried. He must have felt, as he had written in 1830 about his frequent trips to the Paris cemeteries: "So many dead! Why aren't we dead?"

In the beginning of March, Berlioz fell into a coma; his tongue, partially paralyzed, made him appear to smile. He died in the arms of his mother-in-law.

Trumpets blew as they raised the coffin, and at Trinity Church they played excerpts from Glück, Beethoven, Mozart, Cherubini, and Berlioz's own work. Outside the Cimetière de Montmartre, the horses carrying the coffin sud-  denly reared, seizing the bit in their teeth, and running with the coach through the band in front of them, arrived within the gates with Berlioz before the mourners.

[SOURCE: *Berlioz and His Century: An Introduction to the Age of Romanticism*, by Jacques Barzun (New York: Little Brown and Company, 1956)].

*

In his last years, as the crippled old drunk of the Latin Quarter, the violently passionate lover of Rimbaud, with unkempt beard and draped in his disheveled and ragged great coat and red woolen muffler, was highly revered. No matter that the nominal head of the Symbolist movement (he denied his involvement) looked like a vagrant and that he was most often drunk. He was treated by the police, the waiters and the patrons of the places where he dined and drank with complete deference. The artist Frédéric Auguste Cazals, whom, as he would put it today, he had unsuccessfuly tried to "come on to," remained loyal, and occasionally helped to raise money for his friend. Comte Robert de Montesquiou-Fezensac—the model for J.K. Huysmans' De Essientes and Marcel Proust's Charlus—also befriended Verlaine and often served as his patron. Mallarmé kept an admiring and respectful distance, at one point (according to Jean Carrère) turning away to hide his tears upon the café entrance of his extremely drunk friend.

At the hospital Broussais, where Verlaine was forced to spend more and more of his days, Mallarmé, Huysmans, Anatole France, and the young André Gide came to visit him. And there too Verlaine was treated with the greatest of respect. Gabriel Fauré and Claude Debussy had set many of his poems to music. Paul Gauguin had at-

tempted, from Tahiti, to raise money for the great poet. Even Zola, who stood at the very opposite end of the literary spectrum, sent an inscribed copy of La Débâcle to him; Verlaine replied that the book was a masterpiece.

Only the most bourgeoise of writers, such as Edmond Goncourt, described (in the privacy of a journal) Verlaine as a "homosexual murderer." Alphonse Daudet doubtlessly saw him as another example of the rising alcoholism of the French citizenry brought about by the introduction of absinthe through the Algerian wars. And Rémy de Gourmont, the leading Symbolist critic and a founder of Mercure de France, branded him a "bandit." The monocled Leconte de Lisle disdained Verlaine for being a "queer." Verlaine was well aware of these assessments, and even used the rôles of murderer and bandit to his benefit. In 1894 Verlaine was awarded the title of "The Prince of Poets."

Verlaine, however, was not writing great poetry. Living alternately with two prostitutes—the "bad" Esther and the "good" Eugénie, as they were described by friends— he himself swung between the extremes of the disgusting and formidable behavior that had offended Parisian society and occasioned his imprisonment and the sweet saintlessness of his religious evocations, expressed most clearly in Sagesse.

In terrible pain because of an abcess on his leg—early evidence of his syphilitic condition—and almost aways without money enough to eat, Verlaine, like Wilde, had to sell the presence of his company for a few drinks. "When you lead a dog's life, like I do, you must have friends everywhere, and you must have some very strange friends, if only to cover your tracks….If I had enough money to live on, I shouldn't get out of my chair, I should just dream away all the time, with my legs stretched out by the fire. I hate working, I hate talking to people…But I'm poor, you see!"

On January 7th, 1896, Verlaine, who had been ill with fever and gastritis for several days, felt somewhat better. He sent a young disciple, Albert Cornuty, to find Gustave Le Rouge and his mistress for déjeuner. Verlaine drank only a few sips of white wine diluted in water. But the dinner was pleasant. Later that night, he attempted to rise from his bed, but fell to the rug beside it. Eugénie could not lift him, and daring not to wake the neighbors across the way, left him lying on the floor. If true to pattern, she herself was probably drunk. She covered Verlaine with blankets, and with a friend, lifted him, the next morning, back into bed. A doctor was called. A priest from Saint-Étienne-du-Mont heard his confession. At 7:00 that evening Verlaine died. A combination of cir-

rhosis of the liver, diabetes, a heart condition, and syphilis contributed to his pneumonic death.

Two days later, his funeral was held in the church of Saint-Étienne-du-Mont, where Pascal and Racine lie behind the altar. The organist was Gabriel Fauré. Among the mourners were the Parnassians José-Maria de Heredia and René-François-Armand Sully-Prod-homme, Charles de Sivry, Jean Moréas, François Coppée, Maurice Barrès, Verlaine's publisher Jean Vanier, Paul Fort, Robert de Montesquiou, and Stéphane Mallarmé.  *"Verlaine! All your friends are here!" cried Eugénie. Verlaine's body was interred at the Cimetière des Batignolles.*

[SOURCE: *Verlaine*, Joanna Richardson. (New York: The Viking Press, 1971)].

*

Leon had followed me here, to Hanusse, with every intention of putting a bullet through my head. I think he actually imagined it would be a simple thing, in such a small country so easy with sex. But no one seemed to know where I lived. I had moved back into the house—perhaps I should say shack—which my father had built (I think I told you about all that), which had stood so many years people had almost forgotten the place. The postman knew—a man Leon never questioned—and the mayor (who with two *near* pubescent daughters was terrified of outsiders), but few others knew even of my existence. V didn't understand English, and anyway I hadn't hired her on yet. The nurse who helped out—the daughter of an old friend of my mother's, a woman, in fact, who had nursed *me* when my mother died on the very day of my delivery (the doctors proclaimed she had a "bad" heart)—was staying day and night with us. So Leon had no informants to torture out the information from.

Since my arrival—in the off season, when the quay is a cold, dark place where no one waits—I had been into town only once, to buy a goat. Its milk, I was told, was an absolute must since Miss Dukesburry Olivera (the daughter of a Britishman who coupled with her Portuguese mother) was getting quite dried out.

So Leon was up a tree and fit to be tied to the limb at its top. In fact, he blew his metaphorical top by capturing the mayor, who had refused to see him, and taking him to the roof the Parliament house, the tallest building in all of Hanusse, where after much confusion and ineffectual persuasion—(I imagine Señor Domez was so terrified by the questions that he could not understand them; he's also quite forgetful, and could easily have forgotten the informal visit upon repatriation I had bestowed upon him)—Leon threatened to drop him to the street below. In Hanusse you get a crowd for that. Someone had seen him and alerted the soldiers, who, in their inept preparations, alerted the entire populace. According to the postman, who was there, the act took a couple of hours to complete. By that time Leon, affected by the maddened mob below, mistook frenzy for approbation, approval, and encouragement. When the body was tossed, the audience was so appalled it simultaneously pulled apart instead of remaining as a mass, leaving accordingly a hole (as opposed the whole it had just stood as) into which the body splat. It was such an Hanussee thing to do! The mayor was not popular, but this quite transformed this insecure and inert gathering into a vigilante force. Leon was tracked down, arrested and imprisoned the same night.

I testified at his trial, giving evidence of his insanity. We don't kill our prisoners; we torture them to death by the very conditons of imprisonment. I never visited him, but I have heard how the prisoners (all male [women are simply not imprisoned since we recognize that as a culture we have imposed upon them imprisonment enough]) share a series of caves where the strongest of them impose spiritual and sexual trials upon the weaker ones. The mad inhabit two of these interlinking dungeons in the deepest cavities of the "Centre of Incarceration." There, until today, Leon has been locked away.

Not that I have felt compunction for Leon's fate. I only need see Ford and Minnie each day grow to know it was necessary. And I could not have convinced the jurors otherwise, in any event. He *was* mad, he *had* murdered, and *would have* murdered me and probably his own offspring. Did I say *his*? Do you see how still uncertain everything is?

* *
*

The year 1839 was basically a joyful one for Chopin, living as he did in Nohant, the home of his mistress George
Sand, with visitations by Balzac, Delacroix, Louis Blanc,
the singer Pauline Viardot and many others. Chopin,
"the boy" as Sand referred to him, generally went to bed
early, while Sand stayed up to write all night long, retir-
ing as Chopin awoke. During the morning he would com-
pose. It was a time of tranquility—and love.

Now, ten years later, the end of those special years with
Sand still seemed nearly inexplicable. Why had Sand
suddenly turned her pregnant daughter out of the house
and sided against Solange with her son? Why had she
refused nearly all communication with her "little Chip-
Chip"—another endearment she had once used for her
beloved.

For years doctors had pronounced him cured of consump-
tion, but of late he again had been extremely ill, often
coughing up blood. He was always exhausted. The French
Revolution of 1847 had made life even more difficult,
robbing him of most of his pupils and forcing him to
take the offer of his wealthy Scottish pupil, Jane Stirling,

257

to travel to London. British society, however, with all its codes and reserve, and given the fact that Chopin spoke little English, was not to his liking. Musicians were certainly not as celebrated on the British island as they were in Paris, and he could not but want to escape the smothering solicitiousness of Jane and her sister.

He had managed to play a few concerts in Britian, one attended by William Makepeace Thackeray and Jenny Lind. But most of the visit was spent in an exhausting round of social events, which further worsened his physical and spiritual condition.

Back in Paris, however, he was very ill and often without money. Pauline Viardot wrote Sand, begging her to pay Chopin a visit, but Sand merely recounted her incomplete knowledge of the events and, again, portrayed herself as the party subject to Chopin's vituperation and hate. There is little evidence that Chopin ever felt anything other than confusion, hurt, and continued love. In September 1849, Chopin, on advice from his doctors, moved to a new, sunny apartment in Place Vendome. On the evening of October 12th, Chopin's condition worsened, and his doctor summoned the priest. Chopin lived on for four days longer, often in terrible pain. Delfine Potocka traveled from Nice and sang Stradella's "Hymn to the Virgin" for him. Auguste Franchomme and Princess Marceline played Mozart, but their attempt to play his own G minor Cello Sonata was interrupted by a cough which ended in choking.

On the evening of the 16th, Chopin said his last words, "No more." And early the next morning, with his hand held by Sand's daughter Solange, he convulsed and died. A death mask was made by the Polish artist Kwietkowski and a cast of his hands was made by Solange's husband, Jean Baptiste Auguste Clésinger.

More than 3,000 people attended his funeral in the Church of the Madeleine, a funeral paid for by Jane Stirling, humorously referred to as "Chopin's widow." Pauline Viardot and basso Luigi Leblanche sang the Mozart Requiem, as he had at Beethoven's funeral in 1827 and at Bellini's in 1835. The pallbearers included Giacomo Mayerbeer, Auguste Franc-

homme, Eugene Delacroix and Prince Adam Czartoryski.

Chopin's body was buried in the cemetery at Père Lachaise. His heart was cut out and sent to Warsaw to be interred in the church of the Holy Cross.

[SOURCE: *Chopin: The Reluctant Romantic*, Jeremy Siepmann (Boston: Northeastern University Press, 1995).]

*

I am getting quite upset. The Russians have still got Minnie in tow, but where has Ford gotten to? Faraway I hope. For I know that by now Leon knows—has found out—where we live. Clearly Mrs. V had her ears to the ground and just in time, got them out of there. Minnie is my evidence. Perhaps Ford was out wandering and she went to look for him. I hope he didn't return home. I hope…. Useless frets, for I know V would have brought him here to this public place, brought them both. Did I miss him? Wasn't he with the Indians or acrobats? Ahhhh! perhaps she painted him up as a clown—those who at this very moment pass. But none are his height. Could he be the one on stilts?

Another religious procession passes. Reminds me of a funeral. I have been thinking too much of death. To life! I toast my Russian friend who, knowing now who I am, broadly smiles as he returns the declaration. Minne makes a face—still a little mouse in the company of such big rats.

Musicians, row after row. Not a band. Just musicians, mostly violinists and players of the lingo—a flute-like instrument native to Hanusse, but all playing tunes alone, separate, a whirligig of sound. The loudest is an organ grinder who, instead of a monkey, has put a rope to his cat who keeps going off in her own directions. The man must stop from time to time, to pull back.

Of course I'm getting drunk, having been here all the day almost. I have to pee, but can no longer take a chance. I let loose in my pants and a little river runs from under both cuffs. I call the waiter for a new napkin and place it neatly and precise across my crotch as if I am just about to order something up. The waiter is disappointed with my request merely for another glass of wine.

I'm cold now and a little film of sweat has risen across my brow. Here come the ballerinas—a whole cadre—with a retinue of silly boys aleap. Is Ford one of the pretenders to the dance? There is none with his grace.

More clowns, the Indians of this morning, loin cloths barely covering their little dangles of flesh. An erection tightens Dimitri's sailor suit. The same acrobats—we are, after all, a very small nation. Motion is all the tourists ask for, bodies in the act. Some dance along. Others sip mai-tais or martinis in the chairs of the Manango Hotel or—across the street—at the Sheraton —not a hotel of that chain, but a small, dilapidated three story structure that has stolen the name. Everything in Hanusse is from somewhere else. Reminds me of Ricochet's rendition of a philosophical conundrum:

> If the lady is from somewhere
> she is not where she was, for where
> she was is not there when she is where?

*

A breeze rises—that of late afternoon, almost evening—and, as if on cue, hordes of new tourists enter the square to find tables for drinks and the eventual dinner and late-night show. Hula girls return to let the breeze do what it naturally does. I see that some of them are boys beneath, their donning of auburn wigs necessitated, no doubt, by the fact that so many of their sisters are entertaining the tourists in the manner that requires greater bodily contact. Is Ford now a Hawaiian? I do not see his face.

But then much has become a blur as the day suddenly blinks into night. At once, the streetlights, a flood of lights focussed upon the square's center, snap to life, leaving the edges, where most of the sailors sit, in semi-dark. This allows for all kinds of activities that might otherwise have required their coming and going. The cleaning maids perhaps slip into their rooms at this hour. And then, many of the tourists enjoy this lascivious show of shadow and silhouette.

It appears—but this is merely speculation, I admit—that at the Russian table, while one (Aleksandr no doubt) takes the mouse to his lap, the others take on one another, or perhaps they are merely bending to observe more closely Aleksandr's acts—a kind of intense voyeurism at extremely close range. At the Italian table, the shadows represent a mad intermeshing of flesh; at the Greek, a slow dance of undress; the silhouettes of the Romanians seem to slap each other's back; each of the Frenchmen have two heads. It is all a wonder—and utterly terrifying too!

*

263

While we have been watching the slide show, musicians have set up in the corner of the square, and just as suddenly the little band hoots and puffs out a fanfare. Gypsies come running out of every corner, converging in a central ring where they delightfully hurl their bodies into flips and acrobatic leaps. Their women twirl in long colorful dress, while the light plays off their shiny plated bracelets, necklaces and rings in a shower of sparks.

Gradually the tango turns into a muzurka and kozatzkying Russians enter in a long, thin line of hunkering kicks. Some of Minnie's Russians join in, but are too drunk for the gravity of position. One by one, they fall on their faces or backs, bringing forth hoots and howls and laughs.

I alone am unamused, sad. Today has brought on so momentous changes in our lives. A lost daughter, a missing son. For so many years now they have stood for me in a world where I have stood for no one. Now I am just a rusting hull, a stupid drunk. Don't you see, all the ideals we thought we processed were just a ruse for not being who we might have been? Leon offered us a false identity, a passport to the looney-bin or quicker death. That is true, I now know, of all cults, large or small. They are a somewhere to which a person who no one can go to become the someone who can never to return to what he might have become.

And here in Hanusse come an entire pageant of people from the past: Cleopatra, Salomé, Moses, Alexander the Great, Jesus, Uncle Sam, Queen Victoria, Peter Pan, Bugs Bunny, Marie Antoinette, dozens of other dignitaries too. Proust, Verlaine, Berlioz, Chopin, where are they?

*

And where I? You? Lizzie? Suddenly I know where Leon is! What a fool I was—again the utter fool! For they have not let him loose—just let him out! A whip crack and a flourish of trumpet chords accompanies the parade of the prisoners and the insane. They are all tied together in chains and trotted on by billy club-brandishing cops. The whip is just for dramatic effect, for the prisoners, each dragging his body in a direction and pace separate from those to whom they are attached, can hardly move. There is absolutely no possibility of escape! In one of those rows stumbles an old black man, hardly handsome, but with just a few vestiges in nose and jaw of what he might once have been. I am appalled! The man, who used to be Leon, has no being left. Like the others, he is merely a carcass to be pulled in the fray. The whip cracks. They move on. I try to meet his eyes, to see if he has any soul left, but like all the others, he faces only the ground.

So this is the parade of the prisoners I once was told about as a child! I had forgotten this was a ritual here. To trot all those locked away out into public observation once a year. It is a warning and yet a secret admiration for the consequences of their acts. As they pass into a little street just beyond the square, a complete silence descends upon everyone. I am all in tears. O Leon! What did I have to fear?

At that very instant there is a loud cry, a shout. All eyes turn to the tables just outside the light. One of the spotlights is soon swung to the Soviet contingent. A man is lying beside the table with a knife in his side. Dimitri! The beautiful friend. Alexandr has his arm around the neck of our little one, holding her in tableaux. O Hannah, O Hannah, her dress is red, all red, red with what appears to be blood!

266

I tried to run to her, I promise! But I am trapped. I stumble. The police have gotten to her first. I rise, but I am….I can't….I couldn't…I had passed out.

*   *

*

One might say that Alfred de Musset's life had been dominated by strong women. His mother first; then George Sand—with whom he had had a totally tempestuous and almost laughable romantic infatuation beginning in 1833—who had won him away from his mother; then Aimée d'Alton; followed by the great actress of the Théâtre Française Mademoiselle Rachel—"a jewess" as Sainte-Beauve noted; and finally the working girl, Adèle Colin. There were plenty of prostitutes in between, with whom, rumor had it, the dandyish poet and playwright could often behave brutally. He was, after all, alcoholic, and although his hair was still beautifully golden, his face had grown thin, wrinkles punctuating it, with a fleshy lower lip. His clothes, although fastidiously clean, were of another period.

In 1855 and 1856 de Musset went to Hevre for vacation, where he met an English family and two young girls who took a liking to him and even flirted. As he grew ill—a

267

more and more common occurence—the girls sat on the veranda below his window, striking up a friendship with the man above. Some days later, he recovered and prepared to depart. But at the railroad station he found he was missing his trunk, and so missed the train, having to return to the hotel. There he found that the girls had kept it with them to keep him from leaving. He stayed another two days.

Upon his return to Paris he found the calling card of the girls' father. Excitedly, he walked toward their hotel, but turned tail at the door. He was no longer young, no longer well, was now a nervous man old beyond his years. He had been stupid to imagine that he could offer the young girls any but the most miserable of company.

The following year he was sicker. His friend, the playwright Émile Augier, up for election to the Academy, begged Alfred to vote. It was raining and no cab was to be found. Moving slowly under the rue de Rivoli arcade, arm in arm with his brother Paul, he grew short of breath, and had to come to rest every twenty feet. But he arrived just in time to cast the vote that elected Émile. Augier insisted upon a celebration: they should dine at a restaurant and attend a play.

Adèle was outraged upon Alfred's late return, but he was unrepentant. "It may be the last time…. Tattet is calling me." His friend had died a few months previously.

On the 13th of April his heart was acting up, palpitations appearing more and more frequently. De Musset feared that he would be taken to an asylum and begged Adèle to pray. On the first of May he spoke to Paul, summarizing

his loves and hates. Adèle watched through the night. He died the next morning. He was 46 years of age.

At Père-Lachaise he was buried with a tombstone upon which Barre had carved his bust.

[SOURCE: *Alfred de Musset*, Henry Dwight Sedgewick (Indianapolis: Bobbs-Merrill, 1931).]

*

Guillaume Apollinaire, born Guillelmus Apollinaris Albertus de Kostrowitzky in Rome, had become terribly depressed as the woman of his infatuation, Louise de Doligny—his personal version of Proust's Duchesse de Guermantes—grew colder and colder to him, seeing any poet as a virtual failure in life. Apollinaire even threatened suicide. But this period of his military training was a highly creative one, and, as he prepared to go to the front, he turned his attentions to Madeleine Pagès, attempting to recreate in letters an almost carnal relationship. Marriage was proposed, and he even wrote her father asking for her hand. He visited the family in Oran in January 1916.

In March the soldiers prepared for a big attack, and Apollinaire—as does every soldier perhaps—prepared for death. He survived the attack. Back in the trenches he felt lucky to able to continue to read and write. But three days later, while reading the Mercure de France, *he heard a loud nearby explosion and noticed, suddenly, blood pouring over the newsprint. He had been hit in the head.*

The wound at first seemed minor. But, when dizzy spells continued, an operation was ordered. The biographer André Billy went to visit him in the hospital, and was appalled by Guillaume's purple robe. Certainly it did not bode well. The operation, however, seemed to go smoothly. But the convalesence—mostly in Villa Molière in Auteuil—was a long a painful one. His renowned energy seemed to have left him, and a frailness set in. The relationship with Madeleine dissipated.

But just as popular as he was with the literati of Paris, so was he with the nurses. At Auteuil, he met Jacqueline Kolb, who in 1918 he suddenly married.

His return to Paris was a painful one—the city seemed to be so apart from the actualities of the battle. In the press and elsewhere he, as a foreigner, was even faulted for having served at the front. The new generation of young writers, however (Reverdy, Soupault, Cocteau, Breton, Tzara, Albert-Birot) took him up as their hero. And slowly he returned to his involvement in the literary scene, writing poetry, a play, and other works. But his health was never fully restored.

In November, the weekend of Armistice, he and Jacqueline both fell ill to the plague of Spanish Influenza raging through Paris. His condition quickly became serious, as he struggled for breath. "I want to live, I want to live," he told the doctor again and again, "I have so many things to say." Five days later he was dead. His body lies in Père Lachaise.

[SOURCE: *Apollinaire*, Margaret Davies (Edinburgh: Oliver and Boyd, 1964).]

*

Time leaps.

I am in Paris once more, trying to reconstruct the past to make sense of the myth I've spun. The little bar on the Quincampoix has been renovated, and its name changed to—I can hardly believe it—La Russe. The apartment is still. I tried to open its door, but it was locked. I even knocked. But no one opened up.

I went back to my beer. For I know now, I must admit it, you, Elizabeth and you, were never within. Two women sat upon that couch perhaps, but it wasn't the two of you. Leon had gotten others to take your place. I just saw what I wanted. You are truly still in Madrid. The woman in Rome was someone else.

272

But then—I get scared, terribly frightened. Because when I realize the two of you were always dead, I wonder as well whether I am too. Perhaps Leon was not inside, nor Nick. There was no cemetery denouement. The children were traded—or killed perhaps—or maybe they too never came into existence except through my thoughts. Memory is such a mess. You know, I read that the mind can easily be tricked into remembering what never happened. And yet, the person truly believes, honestly testifies to that non-existent event's truth.

Perhaps I was never in Hanusse.

Was there Leon? Was there a war in Viet Nam? The government says we were never "at war." Was there a Holocaust before? Was there us? Was there anyone, the human race? I have no choice but to be unsure. And that is evil, I guess. Our lack of memory, our doubt.

I remember everything now as if it were in a mist.

The jury, I am told, believed Minnie's tale of how the drunken Russian suddenly threatened her life. She was freed—only to be locked away in a convent, some say in Spain, others in Italy. No one will tell me. An abortion was evidently performed, despite the potential religious controversy, in case it might have been the child of that defective human being.

I cannot believe—although I wish I could—that such a lover suddenly turned on a girl with a knife. But I don't want to explore it any further, what he might have said, have told her, to set about that horrible series of events.

Dimitri's body lies in the little Russian cemetery just outside Megos. I have visited it. But then, nowadays, I visit everyones' graves.

*

Carmen *had not been the success that Bizet had hoped for. The critics had been particularly harsh. The failure of the opera, along with domestic problems, led to depression, which he attempted to resist by recalling the better days of his life, the early years of his marriage to the beautiful Geneviève, daughter of his mentor and music teacher, Fromental Halévy. Bizet had then been involved in the early compositions such as the music for Alphonse Daudet's* L'Arlésienne; *and they had lived in an apartment with dear friends and family for neighbors: below them Ludovic Halévy, Geneviève's brother, and his family, and nearby the singer Pauline Viardot and her family, Bizet's dear friends Gounod, Degas, Gustave Doré, Edmond About, and others. Now he felt the very air of Paris was poisoning him.*

Near the end of March he was striken, as he had often been in the past, with a severe attack of throat angina accompanied by acute pain and abesses. Usually he had quickly recovered, but this time the attack went on longer, and when it finally abated, he was left feeling enervated. Gounod, moreover, had returned to Paris in a nervous state brought about by legal battles and his relations with Mrs. Weldon in England. He poured out his rancor to his friend.

Performances of Carmen *continued, under somewhat restricted conditions because Galli-Marié was scheduled to perform in another role, and could not sing Carmen as often. Bizet grew irritable and his tiredness remained. In May his muscular rheumatism intensified, although the idea that he would soon be leaving for the country buoyed his spirits some.*

His doctors disapproved the journey. But Bizet was desperate to leave the city, and on May 28th traveled to Bougival with his wife, his son Jacques (who, along with

275

*his cousin, Ludovic's son Daniel and Robert Dreyfus
would become close friends in preparatory school with
Marcel Proust) and other family members. Georges's
rheumatic pains disappeared. And he and his wife
walked along the river bank, where he later went for a
swim.*

*The next day, however, he had another terrible attack,
and was unable to move his arms or legs. Early Tuesday
morning he suffered a painful heart attack, and a doctor
was sent for from the nearby town in fear of Bizet's im-
minent death. But the crisis appeared to be over.*

*Ludovic arrived on horseback to find his sister in tears
and Bizet still in a high fever. In the middle of the night
Bizet died. Ludovic was called to take his sister from the
house in fear of her nervous condition.*

*The cause of the death was probably a heart attack, al-
though other theories were suggested due to an abscess
in his ear which burst, issuing pus and blood, while Bizet
suffered a coma.*

*Gounod delivered the funeral eulogy at the church of La
Trinité in Paris. The procession to the cemetery at
Montmarte was led by Bizet's father, Gounod, Ambroise*

Thomas, Camille Doucet, Ludovic and Léon Halévy, Massenet and others.

Eleven years later Geneviève married Emile Straus, a rich lawyer connected to the Rothschild family. Mme. Straus's salons and Sunday luncheon parties, along with her personal beauty, wit, and charm made her events extremely popular among the wealthy Parisians, including her young nephew's would-be lover, who used her as a
model for the Duchasse de Guermentes in his A la Recherche du Temps Perdu.

[SOURCE: *Bizet and His World*, Mina Curtiss (New York: Alfred A. Knopf, 1958).]

*

No one. Nothing left. Except this. These words. This little book which has taken me twenty-five years to fill with bits and pieces of paper over which I have

277

scrawled so many little marks in so many different inks. What do these marks mean? Do you see, now, why I wanted Minnie to learn no words. Where has it gotten me? It has led to nothing but a wall of doubt and disbelief.

Mrs. V would not even visit me, in the hospital in Hanusse City where I was taken and kept for so many weeks. Exhaustion, hysteria, alcohol induced amnesia, hemorrhage of the brain, a stroke—the doctors tried out a number of….I cannot remember to word for it; I keep saying "remedies," but it's the opposite I want. The….no not the cure….the cause…the…the definition of what was wrong with me. It's so utterly frustrating! The…*diagnosis*, that's it. The diagnosis. There were many. But still no Mrs. V. No word from anyone. I heard everything long after it had happened.

Isn't it ironic that Minnie, the daughter of such Western sin, should become a nun? And a murderess yet! But then, given all I've written, wasn't this destined? Satan in chains, just like Leon. I can't get rid of that image of him!

Someone exits your building, looking both ways, leaving the door ajar a bit. Hurries away. I am tempted. But I order another beer. I am just imagining things. A woman has left her house. Nothing more. I pay. I walk. There is a little park where I walk, a few feet one way, a few feet the next, a few feet another way, and then the return to gate. I repeat: a few feet one way, a few to the next....

I have only little pleasures. I take a taxi to Père Lachaise.

*

Nijinsky: A Silent Monologue

> [*Nijinsky's wife Romola was just called to the death bed of her husband, who sits up in bed moving his arms as in the ballet,* The Afternoon of the Faun. *His face is transformed, his eyes clear and beautiful again.*]

DOCTOR: *Pray with me for your husband.*

ROMOLA: *What is wrong with him?*

2ND DOCTOR: *His kidneys are gone.*

NIJINSKY: [*seeming to recognize that there are others the room for the first time*] *Mother! Look, look!* [*He gazes off into space.*]

> [*The rest of his speech is to Diagilev, the man so many years his lover and later the one, when Nijinksy married Romola, who destroyed the dancer's career. Romola and the doctors cannot hear him.*]

HE

*HE who I will not say, since HE cannot be sum-
moned. I do not want to summon, do not want to
say. HE is not human. HE is inhuman, a horrific
beast. A beast not to be spoken to, not be be summoned up. But I am not afraid. HE thinks it of me.
HE thinks I am quivering in fear. But I am, as you
see, not quivering here and HE there, wherever HE
may be, is not free. HE is a beast. God has declared it
is wrong to lie down with the cow. I am not afraid. I
do not quiver—except as Eros' messenger sent straight
to the heart of the beast. I do not lie down. Lions lie
down with lambs. I am not a lamb. I am a faun!
Lions don't like to decline anymore than horses do.
But still, they lay. I sit. I stand. I dance! Look! There
is the declension—sit, stand, sway! I will dance away.
The beast is in his lair. The beast is there, nowhere,
hidden beneath the hide of lamb, the kid. I am a faun!
Wolves like fauns, but fauns hate wolves. I do not hate!
I am not afraid. The goat is stubborn. The lion is lazy.
The wolf weary. The faun falls [he collapses upon the
bed, and Romala runs to him].*

*[Suddenly the bed moves from its flat position
to an upended one, so that the following part of*

280

the monologue is delivered with Nijinsky lying flat,
but facing the audience.]
I will shoot the beast as the hunter.
I shall hunt the beast. I shall hunt
The hunter. I shall kill the beast.
I shall caress the beast, carry him away.
I shall take him to my lips and crunch
The beast between the teeth, between the arms,
Crunch his breast between the legs, the thighs,
The cock! HE is the cockerel, a rooster, rooting
Us out. HE creeps. HE is the creep, the creeper
Who creeps into. He is the crack, alack, a snake
Creeping into fact. HE is cra, the cra, cra,
Cra, cra, cra, cra, cra, cra, cra, cra, cra,
The crack, the crap. A crow who comes to sit
On the shoulder. A raven. A craven raven,
A criminal crow, a Crimean crow in crepe
Who creeps into the cockerel. HE is a crook
Whose crime is crowing. HE crawls into the crack
On his back, this black craven raven.
I am the faun, the faux, fool,
Fucked. I am fine. I am divine.
I am the foolish Christ, HE no Christian,
I the Jesus, He the heathen Zeus.
I remorse, HE the torso the criminal

Has taken by force. Peck, peck, peck,
Peck, peck, peck, peck, peck, peck
Upon my neck. Peck upon my neck.
Crow. Creep into my pecker, please!
I will release the seed of your sorrow!
I will let loose a sermon in my semen!
I will free you. I will free me.
For you are HE who cannot be!

[*The bed slowly descends into its flat position again. Romola cries.*]

*

There once was a man, a very large man, who, wherever he went—which was everywhere because everywhere he went there was an event—arrived in style and was naturally sent to the very best rooms and tables and beds, and who was actually underneath all that girth and mirth a little man of utmost seriousness. But no one knew since he was very fat and merry and went everywhere with everyone who was someone to all the affairs and was by everyone who was there seen with everyone else. It was naturally assumed, accordingly, since he laughed a lot and was with everyone else who did too, and was, after a while, friends with everyone else who wanted to, that he was a man with a sense of wit, although he had never said anything much and wouldn't have said even that if he thought someone might have heard what he said. He said "Hello there" and "Why that's quite right" and "I don't know what I was thinking." And "Really" and "My, my" and "Oh, yes." So everyone thought he was very nice.

One day he said "Oh my me" and "No, no!" and "I disagree." And someone observed "You must have gotten up on the wrong side of the bed!" The man, as was normal with him, snorted and laughed and quietly took from a pocket a gun and put it up to the head of the man who said such an utterly stupid cliché. Then he put the gun away.

And afterwards no one for a very long time said anything about him again. And he went no where with no one. He was never seen where anything happened nor where anyone was. And no one said he was clever. And no one said he was big. And no one said he was merry anymore. And no one said he was fat. And he liked that. For he was thin and serious and mean.

But he had to admit it yet, no one knew that.

And over the years some people asked whatever had become of him, the man who was so big, so merry, and witty, who went everywhere with everyone whom they once knew. And so, as time passed, all of them thought it was they who were no longer invited to all the great parties they used to be invited to, and each one felt they had been left out of all the events where things that were so witty and bright took place, and they began to evade the invitations they received and were secretly relieved since they too were actually not very happy and seldom had said something witty or clever. And they were not very nice. The year was 1910, the end of the Nineteenth century.

*   *

*

*The doorbell rang and Victor Hugo was permitted entry
to Balzac's house. "He is dying, sir," cried the servant.
Hugo had come to see his only peer in all of France, and
he went forward past the thousands of objects d'art that
Balzac had collected—despite his terrible finances—to
grace his house and delight his new wife. Eve was not
delighted, but saw them as so much bric-a-brac. But
Hugo saw the vases, the statues, pictures, and cases of
enamel as the proper surroundings for such a great man
as Balzac—and himself.*

*He entered Balzac's room,
encountering a terrible
stench and a monstrous
rattling sound. A nurse
and manservant stood on
either side of the bed, silent, with a look of horror
on their faces. Hugo took
Balzac's sweaty hand.
"He'll die at daybreak,"
said the nurse.*

*Hugo returned down the stairs through the salon and
out the doors into a busy Sunday morning.*

Balzac was buried in Père Lachaise.

[SOURCE: *Prometheus: The Life of Balzac,* by André Maurois, trans. by Norman Denny (New York: Harper & Row, 1965).]

*   *
*

Gertrude had not been feeling well, and in July of 1946 she and Alice left Paris for a country rest. Their friend Bernard Faÿ had offered them his house at Luceau in the Indre-et-Loire. In route Stein began not to feel well. At Azay things had progressed badly enough that they took a room. At an inn they called for the doctor. He told them that she must see a specialist at once. Fearful, Alice called Allan Stein and asked him to meet them at the train station in Paris the next day. The journey seemed endless, and Stein was unable to settle, stalking the compartment and looking out the window at the French landscape. An ambulance was awaiting them, and she was taken to the American Hospital at Neuilly. She was seriously ill, and needed to undergo an operation when she had become strong enough.

The pain became worse, and Stein ordered the doctors to operate despite her condition. She wrote out her will.

286

The operation was scheduled for July 27th, and Alice sat with her awaiting the sedation to take effect. "What is the answer?" Gertrude asked. Alice had had often to remain silent to this powerful woman, and she had no answer. "In that case, what is the question?"

The operation revealed a large cancerous growth. In late afternoon she fell into a coma and at 6:30 was pronounced dead.

She was buried in October (nearly two and a half months later) in Père Lachaise.

[SOURCE: *Gertrude Stein Remembered*, Linda Simon, (Lincoln: University of Nebraska Press, 1994).]

*   *
*

In the little park I walk, a few feet one way, a few feet to the next, a few feet another way, and then the return to gate. When I came out of the coma and could remember things once more, I asked after Minnie and, in particular, after Ford. They told me all about Minnie.

I knew it was a plot, but I kept pretending to myself, it must be because they know nothing. They've not found him yet. Had anyone searched? Was he starving? Living out in the woods like the wild child I always thought he was.

Day after day, no one could tell me anything. I learned to speak again, to walk. How to count, subtract, divide. Gradually, I was getting everything back—except those whom I most loved.

On February 4th, 1995, I was released. I knew what I had to do. I returned to the house. I washed up the dishes, lay Minerva in Minnie's bed, blew out the lights and left.

It takes at least two hours to climb the hilly paths that end in my Tin-Turned Abbey. I was slower now, and it took three. And for the last half hour my heart was all aflutter. Did I expect him to meet me with a smile?

At the little rise, just before you reach the final few feet I saw it all, saw everything, saw and knew why Satan had twice before appeared to me. Just like Adam, what was truly within I perceived without.

For before me I saw the long twist of the metal of what had once been a quonset hut. In a storm or just through the slow erosion of foundation and joints, it had collapsed. I wanted to turn back. I should have, perhaps, but I had to now confirm the awful truth. In his fear, Ford had come to find me, had probably followed me here before, had been the one, perhaps, to know, when I left my little family, where I went. Piecing it together I suddenly realized he was waiting for me here to return as I was waiting for him there to appear.

I crawled over the front end of the hut and climbed across the metal sheets towards the back. Every so often, when I could, I lifted large sheets to peer beneath. Rats ran out. But by the time I reached the far end of the place I was a little bit relieved. I turned back, peeling the sheets, one by one, away again. There was nothing there. Thank heaven. Then I turned back again, repeated these acts. Nothing underneath.

Just a little way beyond where the back wall had stood, however, I saw something strange, two little logs tied at opposite angles, a cross. No name was carved there, but I knew whose grave it marked. I knelt. I wept for a very long while.

But who? Who had found him? Who else had come here too, when I was so convinced no one knew the place? Had V known? Had he shown her the way or had she shown him? Did it matter? They had come here to find me! Did he open the door, enter it, while she stood outside to wait? Or did she go in and report my absence, with Ford darting in to double-check? What's the difference?

I cried. Then I stood to investigate the knot. A perfect sailors'! Where might have V learned that? Ford had been taught by the Portuguese.

Ford. Ford! Just an echo into the woods. Come back! It was all pointless, I knew. Perhaps the Portuguese had also taught a young Nussia the trick.

I began to dig. I dug, first with my hands, but not getting very far, returned home to get the spade. The next morning I dug again, this time deep. The spade hit something more than dirt. I jumped in and pulled it out, not a body, just a little brown box. I opened it. Inside: an empty green bottle which once contained our local beer.

Some say he is in the cemetery of Hanusse City, that Mrs. V is with her family in Megos. Others that I did not dig deep enough. I cannot say anything.

1974–1999

GREEN INTEGER
Pataphysics and Pedantry

Douglas Messerli, *Publisher*

Essays, Manifestos, Statements, Speeches, Maxims,
Epistles, Diaristic Notes, Narratives, Natural Histories,
Poems, Plays, Performances, Ramblings, Revelations
and all such ephemera as may appear necessary
to bring society into a slight tremolo of confusion
and fright at least.

*

Books Published by Green Integer

Green Integer EL-E-PHANT Books
[6 x 9 format]

The PIP Anthology of World Poetry of the 20th Century 1
Edited with a Preface by Douglas Messerli [2000]
readiness / enough / depends / on Larry Eigner [2000]

Books in Preparation

The Peripheral Space of Photography Murat Nemat-Nejat
Operratics Michel Leiris
The Doll and *The Doll at Play* Hans Bellmer
[with poetry by Paul Éluard]
Aphorisms César Vallejo
American Notes Charles Dickens
To Do: A Book of Alphabets and Birthdays
Gertrude Stein
Prefaces and Essays on Poetry
William Wordsworth
Licorice Chronicles Ted Greenwald
Confessions of an English Opium-Eater
Thomas De Quincey
The Renaissance Walter Pater
Venusburg Anthony Powell
Suicide Circus: Selected Poems Alexei Kruchenykh
Captain Nemo's Library Per Olav Enquist
Selected Poems and Journal Fragments Maurice Gilliams
Romanian Poems Paul Celan
The Pretext Rae Armantrout